The Plot to Kill
Susan B. Anthony

Peace,

A novel by William Fleeman

Bill Fleeman

A.K.A.
Art MacDuff P.I.

The Plot to Kill Susan B. Anthony

A novel by William Fleeman

Transformations Enterprises
Cassadaga, NY

Copyright © 2011 by William Fleeman

No part of this book may be reproduced or transmitted in any form or by any means, electronic or mechanical, including photocopying and recording, or by any information storage or retrieval system without written permission from the author, except for brief passages quoted in a review.

ISBN 978-1-882715-15-2

Published by:
Transformations Enterprises
P.O. Box 259
Cassadaga, NY 14718

Disclaimer:
This book is a work of fiction loosely based on historical events. While the famous people named in this book did exist, and Susan B. Anthony did travel and perform many speaking engagements, the plot, and the characters surrounding it are fictitious and do not represent any actual persons, living or dead.

Printed and bound in the USA

Dedication

First, and always first, I dedicate this, my first work of fiction, to my wife Jan, whose exquisite editing skills and loving support led to the publication of three non-fiction books.

I also dedicate this book to those friends and fellow scribes who read the manuscript and gave valuable suggestions.

Peace,
Bill Fleeman

"The people furthest from civilization are the ones where equality between man and woman are furthest apart...No civilization can be perfect until exact equality between man and woman is included."

Mark Twain

Chapter 1

The clock tower across Washington Square Park sounded the hour. Six o'clock, time for me to leave. But as I gathered up my things, I saw someone standing outside the office door reading our sign on the pebble glass window: MacDuff and Davies, Private Investigators.

The person knocked, I opened the door. A Western Union boy had an "urgent message for Mr. MacDuff." I snatched a nickel from my desk drawer, hurried back to the door, and pressed the coin into the boy's hand.

"Thankee, Miss!" He clomped down the stairs, and out the door into the rain.

The telegram showed today's date, Aug 1st, 1891. I opened it.

"MacDuff, it is from Isabella Beecher Hooker," I said.

"Read it to me, Millicent, please!" he rasped. "I'm in no condition…"

I glanced at the brief message and read the first line aloud.

"Will arrive your consulting rooms 9:00 AM tomorrow. Re: matter of life and death."

MacDuff was slumped sideways at his desk, one elbow propped on the desktop, reading an article on Criminal Psychology, and chewing the stem of an old clay pipe. The pipe reeked. MacDuff had said, earlier, that there was a little bugger inside his head wearing steel toed shoes, and he was trying to kick out the walls of MacDuff's skull. MacDuff claimed to be suffering, in his words, from perhaps "the worst hangover of the millennium!" He was trying to decide whether to extend a three-week bender that had begun the day after we solved our most recent case.

I saw MacDuff's hand inch toward the bottom drawer where he kept the bottle. He lifted the bottle half way out of the drawer as I read the rest of the message.

"Oh my god, MacDuff! Someone is plotting to kill Susan B. Anthony!"

The bottle thumped back down in the drawer.

"The famous Suffrage lady," MacDuff rasped.

"None other," I said.

Leaning on the desk to steady himself, MacDuff got to his feet. He closed his dark brown eye, stared at me from out of the icy blue one.

"Millicent, we can't wait till we see Mrs. Beecher Hooker tomorrow morning, we've got to do something now. If a real plot exists, Miss Anthony's life could damn well depend on how fast we get moving."

MacDuff looked at his watch.

"Well, it's too late to knock on anybody's door tonight. Especially as I probably don't look, uh, exactly too presentable right now. I mean, to be talking to people maybe in their parlor."

I told him he was right.

"But it's not too late to visit Justus Schwab's Saloon, Millicent, so let's go!"

I knew the idea of going to Justice Schwab's was not a ploy to start another binge. MacDuff never drank when on a case -- never. In fact, we often began a new case with a visit to Justice Schwab's.

"Well," I said, "if anybody in Manhattan knows about a plot to kill Miss Anthony, someone at Justice Schwab's probably would."

"But, Millicent, please, first you have to help me get well."

Earlier that day I tried to persuade him to go and sweat it off at Hoffmeister's Gym, where he lifted weights and boxed. He refused, mumbling something about the sound of barbells banging together.

We entered MacDuff's private quarters through the door at the back of the office. MacDuff grabbed some cold ham out of the icebox, and slapped the ham between two slabs of bread while I boiled the coffee. After eating, he donned a fresh black silk shirt and bohemian style floppy bowtie, also black.

"Well, Millicent?" MacDuff said. He held out his right hand. "Steady as a rock, see?"

"You'll do, MacDuff." There was just the slightest tremor.

Glancing out the rain-streaked window I saw a cab standing at the curb across the street. It was raining hard. I threw on my cape, grabbed my bag and umbrella. MacDuff put on a jacket.

Turning down the gas, we locked the office door, hurried down the stairs, and out, then dashed across the street through the cold rain. It felt more like an early October night, than one in early August. I pulled my cape closer round me.

MacDuff pounded on the side of the cab, waking the driver who was snoozing inside out of the rain. He jumped out, crammed his hat on his head, and climbed up onto the open driver's seat in back. Closing my umbrella, I got in and sat down on the tufted leather seat. MacDuff followed. He slid open the little communicating door in the roof of the cab.

"Justus Schwab's Saloon, number Fifty, 1st Street!" he yelled.

"And hurry, driver! I shouted, sliding the door shut.

Chapter 2

We rattled down the streets through the rain towards Justus Schwab's, hoping to see someone there who could help us. As we were entering the saloon, a very drunk man staggered out. We stood aside to let him pass. Holding the swing door open, MacDuff swept off an imaginary hat, bowed, and said to the drunken man:

"'That men should put an enemy in their mouths to steal away their brains.'" The quote MacDuff used from Shakespeare was what I had often used against MacDuff, when he was in the condition of the drunken man who lurched past.

As usual it was noisy and crowded inside, but Justus Schwab's is not a dive. You enter the saloon at street level, and you are not served needled beer doctored with benzene, or some other poison. MacDuff and I went in. The waitress came to seat us.

"There, Rene." MacDuff pointed to a table for two in a corner in back, where the gas was not so high nor the conversation so loud.

Rene wiped our table. "What would you like this evening, Miss Millicent?"

"I shall have a beer, I think, Rene."

"And you, MacDuff?"

MacDuff hesitated. I touched his shin under the table with the toe of my shoe.

"Uh, make mine coffee," MacDuff said. "Straight-up, no chaser."

"Ah, then you must be working." Rene said.

MacDuff and I studied the faces in the crowd. Self-proclaimed socialists from German Town, proud anarchists from Jew Town, exiled revolutionaries from Russia and France hiding out in Little Italy.

We recognized a man sitting talking at one of the tables just inside the saloon front door. He had come in moments after we arrived. Robert Johnson, a US Congressman from New York who lived in one of the uptown wards. Johnson, a slender older man, was conversing with a well-dressed man standing next to the table with his back to us. I thought he looked like another politician. Neither of us had much use for politicians. But for an Uptown politician, Johnson enjoyed a good reputation among the denizens of lower Manhattan. Because he claimed to be a friend to the poor, also because he publically supported liberal causes such as free birth control for the poor. He also claimed to be a friend to Miss Anthony, and had always said that he supported Suffrage.

"Actually," I said, "I think Congressman Johnson is a likable man, that is, for a politician."

MacDuff pretended to gag.

Likable or not," MacDuff said, "I don't trust any politician. I trust the ones I like, even less."

Glancing round the smoky saloon, I saw someone else I recognized. "Look, MacDuff," I said.

"Emma Goldberg."

"I saw her, Millicent."

"But who is the man with her?"

"Alexander Berkholdt," MacDuff said.

"Ah, her paramour. They've been together but a short time, I believe."

Emma Goldberg and Alexander Berkholdt, sitting at a table nearby, were well-known anarchists who came often to Justus Schwab's Saloon to talk politics with other Lower Manhattan radicals who hung out there. Berkholdt shot a look our way, then whispered something to Miss Goldberg.

"If anybody knows anything, those two would," MacDuff said, keeping his voice low.

Just as Rene returned with MacDuff's coffee and my beer, Emma Goldberg and Alexander Berkholdt got up from their table and wove a zigzag path through the crowd toward the rear of the saloon.

"MacDuff, look." I pointed at the retreating figures.

"Damn!" he said. "I want to talk to those two."

MacDuff jumped up and went after them. When the two anarchists bolted out the back door, he ran out too. A couple of minutes later he returned. Catching Rene's eye, he motioned her over to the table.

"Rene, it's real important that Millicent and I talk to Emma Goldberg and Alexander Berkholdt."

"They just left by the back door."

"I know, Rene. I followed them, but by the time I got out in the alley they were gone. Any idea where they went?"

"Probably, they went home."

"Where's that?"

"Jew Town, they have a flat."

"Exactly where?"

"One of the tenements, third floor, I think. I was there once -- say, MacDuff, why do you want so bad to see Emma and Alex?" Rene gave MacDuff a look.

"We need their help on a case."

"It's true, Rene," I said. "A sister's life has been threatened."

"Who -- what sister's life?" She stepped closer to the table.

"We cannot tell you her name," I said. "But we can tell you this, Rene. You would not want this sister to die. She is a powerful friend to the New Woman." I opened my purse and took out a note pad and pen, and set them on the table.

Rene glanced round the saloon. She wrote something on the pad, and hurried away.

"Rene!" MacDuff yelled at Rene's back. "What's the chance of catching them home tomorrow?"

Rene shouted over her shoulder, "Unless there's some kinda big anarchist rally somewheres, they'll be home alright."

MacDuff looked at his watch, then stood up. "Okay, Millicent," he said. "Might as well go home, rest up. We've got a long day ahead of us tomorrow."

MacDuff left too much money on the table for our drinks. I snatched my note pad and Waterman off the table, hoisted my umbrella from the back of the chair, and went with MacDuff to the door. Robert Johnson, the Uptown politician, and his friend had also left the saloon.

Outside Justus Schwab's it was still raining hard, and now a strong wind blew from the East River. A sudden gust turned my umbrella inside out. MacDuff ran down to the corner to hail a cab while I waited under the awning. A hansom stood across the street, the driver huddled under his raincoat with his back to the wind and rain. MacDuff stepped off the curb. He cupped his hand to his mouth ready to call out to the cabbie.

Precisely at that moment, a black coach sped past Justus Schwab's. Throwing jets of water from its wheels, the coach swerved round the corner straight at MacDuff. I screeched! MacDuff jumped clear. The coach raced south down Broadway. I ran to the corner fast as I could, and I grabbed MacDuff's arm.

"MacDuff! Are you alright?" My hand shook.

"Phew!" he said. "Yeah, I'm okay. He looked at me. "I've been shot, stabbed, and sapped, Millicent," he said. "But nobody ever tried running me over in a four-wheeler before. Say, you sounded like one of those opera hall sopranos. Or a Cherokee screech owl, I'm not real sure which."

Gently, I poked him in the ribs with my elbow. He grinned. A shiny wedge of straight black hair fell down over his brown eye. The blue one caught the light from the street lamp.

"MacDuff! That coach had no side lamps."

"It had lamps, alright, they just weren't lit."

We stood in the rain and watched the coach disappear down Broadway.

"There was something else about that coach and matched pair, MacDuff."

"Yeah. They didn't make any noise. I didn't hear the coach, didn't hear the horses."

"Why didn't we hear anything, on a night like this with no other traffic on the street?"

"Rubber tires, Millicent, and rubber horseshoes. I've used the trick myself."

"It was no accident, MacDuff." He put his hand on mine.

"I know, Millicent. They meant to kill me."

Chapter 3

The cab was still at the curb. We walked unhurriedly across the street. Now the cabbie was wide-awake.

"It was yer scream what waked me, Miss," the cabbie said.

"Washington Square," MacDuff said. "Number twenty-six 4th Street."

We climbed in and settled back. We were chilled to the bone, and my teeth chattered.

"MacDuff?"

"Yeah."

"Obviously, someone knew Mrs. Beecher Hooker was going to contact us. Someone wants us out of the way, MacDuff."

"Yeah, wonder why, Millicent? And I wonder how they knew we were there."

"They must have followed us here. MacDuff, I wonder why Emma Goldberg and her paramour ran out when we came in Justice Schwab's."

"After we talk with Mrs. Beecher Hooker in the morning," MacDuff said wearily, "we'll go and see them."

When we climbed out of the cab in front of our building, it had stopped raining. We said goodnight in the foyer, and MacDuff climbed the stairs to his rooms on the second floor. I had inserted my key and was unlocking the door to my first floor flat, when MacDuff called to me. I looked up.

"Millicent," he said. Then after a pause, "Thanks."

"Don't mention it, MacDuff."

I opened my door and put my key back in my bag. Then I turned and looked up again at MacDuff, who was now at the top of the stairs.

"MacDuff."

He stopped and stood with his back to the hall lamp, his shadow filling the foyer.

"Why do you do it, MacDuff? I mean, you might have been killed tonight."

He did not answer.

There was another woman in MacDuff's life, of whom I am exceedingly jealous. I blame her. Look for her the next time you walk past the courthouse. She's the blindfolded woman standing at the courthouse door. She holds a balance scale in one hand, a short sword in the other.

Students of Greek Mythology call her the Goddess of Justice. To MacDuff, she is simply the Blind Lady. That's who he risked his life for tonight outside Justice Schwab's Saloon.

MacDuff climbed to the top of the stairs. I heard his door open, then close. Inside my flat I prepared for bed. Before tuning down the gas, I glanced at myself in the mirror.

"You are a rather comely specimen of Victorian womanhood," I said aloud to the image in the glass, "far more handsome than that woman made of stone."

I might have had bad dreams that night, but did not thanks to the tonic of laudanum I drank before retiring.

My last thoughts before the laudanum took effect were of MacDuff. How did this enigmatic part-Cherokee Indian man with a fifth-grade formal education, who understands the nuances of Greek Philosophy better than most University trained scholars -- how did such a man become an expert in the field of criminal psychology? And how did I become this enigmatic part Indian man's partner?

"Good night, MacDuff," I said aloud in the darkness of my room. "'…and flights of angels sing thee to thy rest…'" Then I fell down, down, down into sweet, sweet laudanum dreamland.

Chapter 4

The August sky was overcast in the morning, and a light rain was falling. As I went around turning up the gas, I heard coach wheels scrape the curb in front of our building. Looking out of the window, I saw the driver climb down and open the coach door. An elderly woman prepared to step out. I glanced at the clock on the mantle. Nine o'clock, she was right on time.

The driver took the woman's arm and helped her down. Holding an umbrella above her head, he shut the coach door and helped her across the cut stones. She raised her skirts not quite to the tops of her high button shoes, and leaning heavily on a stout cane limped to the door.

"It is she, MacDuff!"

MacDuff cast his eye along the length of the room.

"Millicent, this place is a mess!"

The place was, indeed, a mess.

MacDuff swept news clippings, notebooks, pens, and other debris from his desktop into a deep drawer. He wadded up newspapers strewn about on the floor by the hearth and stuffed them into the coalscuttle. I grabbed a dozen books piled on tabletops and chairs all over the room, and crammed them any old way into the bookcase next to MacDuff's desk. I brushed cigarette ends and ashes from my desk blotter into the ashtray and emptied it in the hearth. I lifted MacDuff's gray cat Shadow from the hearthrug, opened the door to MacDuff's private quarters, dropped the cat inside and re-closed the door.

There came a polite knock. I opened the door. Standing in the hallway dressed in Victorian basic black was the short, stout figure of Mrs. Isabella Beecher Hooker. A strand of white hair poked out from her bonnet. Her driver, a tall middle-aged man stood at her side shaking raindrops from his bowler.

"Mrs. Beecher Hooker, I am so pleased to meet you!" I said.

"And who are you, my sister?"

"My name is Millicent. Please, do come in."

Mrs. Beecher Hooker stepped into the consulting room.

"So, you are Mr. MacDuff's assistant?"

"No, my partner."

I had not seen MacDuff come and stand next to me.

"Oh!" said Mrs. Beecher Hooker. "What a pleasant surprise."

"How so?"

"That your partner is a woman, Mr. MacDuff."

He shrugged.

"I know that Mr. Pinkerton would never employ a woman. Although it is upon his recommendation that I am here to consult with you. Pinkerton does hold you in high esteem, Mr. MacDuff. When I saw him yesterday, he said, 'MacDuff is the best private investigator in the business.'"

There was a long silence. MacDuff served his private investigator's apprenticeship as a Pinkerton Man. But Pinkerton and MacDuff had some strong disagreements over the course of a year or two. Finally, Pinkerton fired him, so MacDuff opened his own private investigator agency. It was just before I meet him. Of course, since I am a woman, I cannot obtain my own official PI license but I am allowed to work under MacDuff's.

"I'm pleased to meet you, Mrs. Beecher Hooker." MacDuff grasped her hand. "And you, sir," he said to the driver who stood in the hall. "C'mon in. Hang your wet stuff there." MacDuff pointed with his chin at the clothes tree next to the door.

I offered Mrs. Beecher Hooker one of the chairs next to the hearth. She sat down, setting her purse next to her. She folded her hands on top of her cane and rested her chin on her hands.

It was unusually chilly for a summer morning, so MacDuff had laid a small fire in the hearth. MacDuff and I sat on the settee facing Mrs. Beecher Hooker. The driver occupied the window seat next to the clothes tree.

"Oh, my," Mrs. Beecher Hooker said, looking closely at me. "You do remind me of Susan! When she was a young woman, that is. You are about her height, I should think." Mrs. Beecher Hooker stage-whispered into her hand, "But my dear, you are prettier, by far, and I see that you do not need a corset. And I do adore your hair, so shiny black."

I accepted her compliments with a smile.

MacDuff leaned forward. "Mrs. Beecher Hooker, you said in your wire that someone could be plotting to kill your friend Susan B. Anthony."

"Yes, although I would rather it were my life that was in jeopardy." Mrs. Beecher Hooker sighed. "But, Mr. MacDuff, there is no could be about it."

She opened her purse and removed an envelope. MacDuff gave me a nod. I took the envelope, removed the single page, and read the message, silently.

It was brief:

> "Make no mistake, Miss Susan B. Anthony must die. Should she live to see the leaves fall...."

MacDuff and I studied the message together. It was typed on an older machine and, though brief, the letter showed signs that the author was an educated man or woman. I had noticed, as we read, that the paper was not of common grade. It was unusually thick, and expensive. I pointed out to MacDuff that some of the typewriter keys had pierced the thick paper.

"Looks like the typist has a heavy hand," MacDuff said.

The message was unsigned, the envelope cancelled by a clerk in the Main Post Office at Broadway and Park Row.

"Millicent?"

"Yes?"

"The envelope, look at the backside."

"Black sealing wax."

We all knew what that meant. No one in 1891 used black sealing wax except when sending a death notice. Our would-be assassin had a flair for the dramatic.

"But why would the writer be so stupid as to give advance notice of a killing?" I said.

"Yeah, strange isn't it, Millicent," MacDuff said.

"The assassin, if he's the one who wrote the letter, is what your English relatives call a sporting man. Whoever he is, he'll make a bundle of money for pulling the trigger. But some people who kill for money often have another motive. Maybe our man kills as much for the thrill of it, as for the money. The money's important, yes, but people like the one who wrote that letter get drunk on the thrill of murdering someone, and getting away with it. But the job can't be too easy, otherwise there wouldn't be enough of a thrill."

We determined that the person who wrote the letter might live somewhere in Lower Manhattan. Of course, we agreed that he could hail from Chicago, or Dallas, or San Francisco, even London or Paris, with an accomplice in New York City who received the letter and then re-mailed it from the Manhattan Post Office using a new envelope.

MacDuff looked at Mrs. Beecher Hooker. "I suppose you've shown the letter to Miss Anthony?"

"Yes. Miss Anthony is staying in New York just now with friends. I went to see her before I came here, but I did not tell her I would be consulting a detective."

"How'd she take it, when you showed her the letter?"

"As I thought she would, Mr. MacDuff. She smiled, and with a wave of her hand dismissed the matter. 'Not worth bothering about, Belle,' she said."

Of course, MacDuff and I knew this wasn't the first time someone had threatened to harm Susan B. Anthony. We knew that she had had things thrown at her, and had been burned in effigy. On one occasion, a life-size cardboard image of Miss Anthony had been dragged through the streets of Boston behind a Hansom cab. Recalling these events, Mrs. Beecher Hooker shook her head in disgust.

"And twenty years ago," said Mrs. Beecher Hooker, "when Miss Anthony spoke in a park in Rochester, New York, her home town, mind you! A man in the crowd said he'd 'a mind to hang her by the neck from one of the trees.'"

"How did Miss Anthony respond to that threat?" I said.

Mrs. Beecher Hooker smiled. "She didn't blink an eye, Miss Millicent. She simply ignored the man. Of course, nothing came of the threat," Mrs. Beecher Hooker said. "The man walked away in a huff, and that was the end of it."

I could not help smiling. I had heard of Miss Anthony's fearlessness.

"Have you gone to the police yet?" MacDuff said, waving the letter like a flag.

"Oh no!" Mrs. Beecher Hooker rearranged her skirts. "Miss Anthony," she said, "is a woman of single-minded purpose, Mr. MacDuff."

She explained that Miss Anthony had only one thing in her mind at all times, to raise the Suffrage flag, and keep waving it until all women were given the right to vote. Mrs. Beecher Hooker said that Susan would never forgive her if she went to the police.

"Nor," she added, "would Susan ever forgive me if she discovered that I had consulted not just one, but two private detectives."

"But Miss Anthony's life is in imminent danger," I said, "and surely the cause of Woman's Suffrage would be delayed fifty years if anything happened to her now!"

According to Mrs. Beecher Hooker, Miss Anthony would never accept that line of reasoning, and would never agree to involve the official police. She said Miss Anthony knows the value of publicity, but believes that in this case the publicity would bring far greater harm to the Suffrage cause than would her own death. She believes that many people would hesitate to attend Suffrage events, lest something happen to them.

"Besides," Mrs. Beecher Hooker said, "she does not believe the threat is a serious one."

MacDuff shook his head.

"So Miss Anthony thinks the person who wrote this death threat, that's what it is, Mrs. Beecher Hooker. Make no mistake, it is a death threat," MacDuff said. "But she thinks the person who wrote it is just some kind of crackpot, is that it?"

"Yes. Crackpot. She chose that exact word! 'He's a crackpot,' she said, whose threats would come to nothing." Mrs. Beecher Hooker paused. "Do you suppose she might be right, Mr. MacDuff?"

MacDuff stared at her. "Mrs. Beecher Hooker," he emphasized each word, I don't take chances with anybody's life."

MacDuff stood up. He paced back and forth in front of the hearth, and then sat down again.

"Where is Miss Anthony staying?"

"With Doctor Lozier and her family, in West 48th Street. But, please, Mr. MacDuff, I beg of you, do not go there to interview Susan."

"Right now I can't think of any reason we'd want to," MacDuff said.

"Belle," I said, "exactly why is Miss Anthony in New York right now? Can I call you that, Belle?"

"Oh, please do!"

"And I'm MacDuff, forget the mister."

"Just call me Millicent," I said.

"Susan will soon begin a speaking tour on Suffrage that will take her across New York State. That is why she is here right now. She will do the first speech in Brooklyn."

"Where in Brooklyn, and when? And where will she go next?"

Belle opened her purse and looked inside. "Oh, yes, here it is." She removed a clipping.

"Her schedule," she said, handing the clipping to me. "It was in the *New York Sun* this morning."

"MacDuff," I said, "Miss Anthony's first engagement is eight o'clock in the evening, day after tomorrow, at the College of Psychic Studies in Brooklyn."

MacDuff and I looked at each other.

"Yes, that is correct." Belle smiled. "Most of the members of the college are Spiritualists. Miss Anthony does not, herself, believe very much in that sort of thing, but organizations such as the College of Psychic Studies welcome Suffrage workers when other more conservative institutions will not allow us through their doors."

"Where does she go next?" MacDuff asked, looking at me. I looked at the list. "To Poughkeepsie."

"Her very last speech will take place in Lily Dale, New York," Belle said, excitedly.

MacDuff and I gave each other another look.

Belle smiled. "Another Spiritualist organization. Lily Dale is a Spiritualist summer camp about fifty miles west of Buffalo, near the Pennsylvania border."

"Belle," I said. "You told us that you went to the Pinkerton agency before you wired us. I take it the Pinkerton agency suggested that you contact our office."

"Yes, they felt the job was more in your line of business."

"I see."

That could explain, I thought, how the person driving the coach that almost ran MacDuff down knew that we would be on the case. Surely Miss Anthony's would-be assassin knows enough about her to guess that she would not want the plot to become public knowledge. Also, he would know that Miss Anthony's friend Mrs. Beecher Hooker would respect Miss Anthony's wishes.

Obviously, the person who wrote the letter, or one of his agents, shadowed Mrs. Beecher Hooker from the time she got the letter. He followed her to the Pinkerton Agency, and someone there told him that Mrs. Beecher Hooker was going to hire us. Surely the assassin, or his agent if he has an accomplice, would check on that. Undoubtedly, he staked out our office. Last night he followed us to Justice Schwab's Saloon, and then taking advantage of the situation, he decided to eliminate MacDuff while he had the chance.

Once more, MacDuff held the letter up.

"It's not much to go on," he said, "but it'll have to do for now."

"Then you will take the case?"

MacDuff and I nodded affirmatively. Mrs. Beecher Hooker beamed.

"Millicent and I have contacts in Lower Manhattan, people who might know something about a plot to kill Miss Anthony. We'll start our investigation by interviewing those contacts. In fact, we've already started, as of last night."

Belle tensed. "I do worry that one of your contacts might

cause the plot to become public knowledge."

"Belle," I said. "You needn't worry. No one MacDuff and I interview would tell the official police, or the press, anything about this matter. They wouldn't dare, Belle." I pointed at MacDuff.

MacDuff had the envelope and letter still in his hand. He had closed his brown eye. The blue one glittered like a chip of ice. He stared at the black sealing wax on the back of the envelope, and drew back his lips. Belle shivered. The three of us sat very still, a sort of tableau.

Belle leaned forward, breaking the spell. "There is one more thing, your fee, MacDuff."

"Never mind about that for now. As I said, we'll interview some reliable sources. People we can trust, who might have heard of a plot to kill Miss Anthony, or even a rumor of one. We'll continue our investigation tomorrow morning, then meet with you at your hotel some time in the afternoon. By then we can give you a better idea about fees and expenses.

"It could add up to a lot of money, Belle, if we can't clear this thing up before Miss Anthony leaves New York City. We might have to follow her all the way across New York State. If so, then we'd have to hire one, maybe two deputy agents to help with surveillance."

"My dear Mr. MacDuff." Belle breathed deeply. Her shoulders slumped. "My friend Susan's life is at stake. Her safety is all I care about and I insist on giving you and Millicent a retainer for your services. I believe it is customary, is it not?"

MacDuff gave a wave of his hand to dissuade Belle, but she paid him no mind. She opened her purse and withdrew some money. She counted out five hundred dollars and handed the money to MacDuff. He shrugged, took the money and handed it to me. I locked it in the cash box in my desk.

I helped Belle with her coat. Her driver, John, woke from his nap on the bench by the window.

At the door, Belle whispered, "Please come out in the hall with me, just for a moment." I followed her out.

"What is there about his eyes, Miss Millicent?"

"It is a rare occurrence, Belle. MacDuff was born with one brown eye, and the other blue."

Belle smiled. "Rather distinctive, I should say. One of Susan's eyes wanders a bit."

Mrs. Beecher Hooker smiled, and left our office. I did not feel like smiling. I was concerned, no, worried. No, scared is the better word.

Chapter 5

The address Rene had scribbled down at Justus Schwab's, although not exact, was close enough for a start. She had written 'Hester Street tenement, near Mott.' We walked east on Grand to Centre Street. MacDuff and I were familiar with that part of Lower Manhattan, MacDuff more than I because he grew up there.

"Lower Manhattan," I mused. So much like Whitechapel or Stepney, London's East End where lived the poorest of England's poor.

"It's been a long time since I've been in this neighborhood," MacDuff said. "It hasn't changed much."

MacDuff held his nose and pointed to high mounds of garbage piled along the curbs. He waved at a group of dirty faced kids playing stoopball.

An old man with a pushcart stood on the other side of Centre Street, selling apples and pears. We crossed the street, and MacDuff bought two pears from the old man. The old man grinned, showing no front teeth. He said something to MacDuff in Yiddish. MacDuff laughed his quiet Indian laugh. When MacDuff was a kid living on the streets, the old man let him steal apples from his pushcart.

We both had a working knowledge of the Eastern European languages spoken in Lower Manhattan. MacDuff, as I said, grew up there. I owe my knowledge to my years of expensive education in Europe, provided by my parents before my father gambled away my mother's fortune, and then killed himself.

Also there was my acting career, another of my avocations. I have played mostly minor parts in houses on Lower Broadway, where all the seats are cheap and the stage more accessible to a part African immigrant woman. I learned to communicate with fellow actors from many immigrant groups.

MacDuff asked the old peddler whether he knew Emma Goldberg and Alexander Berkholdt, and whether he knew where they lived. At the mention of Berkholdt's name, the old man paled.

He glanced over his shoulder, looked both ways up and down Centre Street, and lowering his voice said something to MacDuff in Yiddish. MacDuff nodded to me.

The old man had given him the information we needed. As we turned to leave, he caught MacDuff's coat sleeve. He leaned close to MacDuff, and I heard him say, "You be careful, my friend. Alexander Berkholdt, I hear he once kill a man."

We walked east off Centre Street onto Hester. This was the open marketplace the Irish and Italians a few blocks away jokingly called the Pig Market, because it was in Jew Town and the one thing you couldn't find there was pork. Walking along the street, MacDuff and I heard fierce arguments over the price of an orange, and the merits of a scrawny chicken. Soon we came to a large tenement house. We turned down an alleyway.

Paved with broken cobblestones and littered with garbage, the alleyway led to a small central court. A water hydrant with a pump grew out of the cobblestones back in a corner of the court. The hydrant supplied drinking water for the tenants living in the surrounding buildings. Right next to the water hydrant stood a row of privies. The privies reeked.

Bed sheets and clothing hung high above our heads on clotheslines strung across the court between the wooden buildings. As we started towards the stairs that led to the upper two stories, MacDuff grabbed my arm.

"Look," he said.

I spied the brim of a bowler hat sticking out of the entryway to the stairs. I saw one eye and one ear under the hat, and then MacDuff and I both saw a slender man of average height turn and run up the stairs.

We climbed the rickety stairs to the third floor. Reaching the landing, we heard a door slam shut somewhere nearby. We tiptoed down to the end of the dimly lit hallway, stopped and faced a closed door. Was the man on the stairs now standing behind this door, with a gun in his hand? We each stood against the wall, on either side of the door. Opening my bag, I removed my revolver and held it at my side. MacDuff removed his revolver from the underarm holster, tucked it in his belt and re-closed his coat.

MacDuff reached out his hand and knocked on the door. Footsteps approached.

"Yes?" A woman's voice.

"Is Mr. Berkholdt in, Mr. Alexander Berkholdt?"

"Who would want for to know?"

"My name is MacDuff."

"And why to Mr. Alexander Berkholdt do you wish to speak?"

"My words are for his ears only."

"What, may I be so boltd to ask, is your business, Mr. Mac Duff?"

"I'm a detective."

There was a long silence.

"A private detective," MacDuff said.

The bolt slid back. The door opened, revealing a short solidly built woman in her early twenties. She had on a high-necked white blouse with puffy sleeves, the blouse tucked neatly inside her long brown skirt. I moved to MacDuff's side.

The woman smiled. "You will please to come in."

MacDuff and I stepped inside. Like most of the flats in Lower Eastside tenements, there were two tiny rooms, one behind the other. No one else was in the room we had just entered. The woman threw back her head and thrust out her bosom.

"My name is Emma Goldtberg." she announced dramatically, giving the 'd' a hard 't' sound.

I drew myself erect, and threw back my head. And thrust out my bosom, although as bosoms go mine was not as remarkable as Miss Goldberg's.

"I am pleased to meet you, Miss Goldberg," I said. "My name is Millicent."

"You, my sister Millicent, and you, Mac Duff, please to call me Emma."

The three of us shook hands. Emma's hands were rough and calloused, her handshake as strong as a man's. She saw me wince as she released her grip.

"Oh, my sister," she said. "I am so sorry. It is my work at the mill. My hands, you see, they are large and strong. I forget sometimes to shake hands more like lady."

She closed the door. She threw the bolt, which made me uneasy.

We now stood in Emma's combined kitchen and sitting room, sparsely furnished but exceptionally neat and clean. A square wooden table stood at the center of the room. Beyond the table, directly opposite the entrance, was the door that gave on the bedroom. That door was closed. A coal-burning cook stove stood against the right-hand wall. A single tall window set in the left-hand wall faced the court below.

Emma invited us to sit down at the table, insisting that I take the chair facing the closed door. It was more comfortable, she said. I felt MacDuff's hand on my elbow.

"No, no, Millicent, let me take that chair. You'll like this chair better," he said.

I sat down on the chair facing Emma. MacDuff sat in the chair facing the closed door. Emma did not see MacDuff remove his revolver from his belt as he sat down, but I did. Moreover, I knew MacDuff's revolver, out of sight, now, under the table, pointed directly at the closed door.

Emma rested her hands on the table; her fingers laced tightly together, the knuckles showing white. She cleared her throat…

Chapter 6

The closed door flew open! A man with a revolver stood in the opening, the gun aimed at MacDuff's chest. Of medium height, with dark hair combed straight back from a high forehead, he stepped quickly into the room. Alexander Berkholdt, of course.

He stared at MacDuff through gold-rimmed spectacles. Now MacDuff's revolver pointed at Berkholdt's groin.

Berkholdt cocked his revolver -- 'snap!'

MacDuff's .38 answered -- 'snap!'

Berkholdt's face paled.

My heart skipped. Emma Goldberg stopped breathing.

"Who are you? And who sent you?" Berkholdt demanded.

"We're who we say we are," MacDuff said. "Two private detectives working on an important case. I'm MacDuff, she's Millicent. Nobody sent us, we're here because we need your help."

"What is this important case that you think Miss Goldberg or I could help you with?" Berkholdt tightened his grip on the revolver.

Without taking his eyes off the man or the gun, MacDuff nodded to me.

"Mr. Berkholdt," I said, "someone has threatened to kill Susan B. Anthony. A close friend of Miss Anthony hired us to stop the assassin."

Berkholdt's eyes opened wide. "But who would want to kill such a woman?"

"Yes! Miss Anthony is worker not only for the Suffrage! She stands for rights of women who slave in factories but receive only half wages of men." Miss Goldberg shouted, leaning forward.

"And I fight at my Emma's side, and Miss Anthony -- she is our sister in the glorious Cause!" Berkholdt yelled.

"Yes! Miss Susan Anthony is woman of the people. Is true revolutionary -- is comrade!" Emma shrieked.

Miss Goldberg's loud enthusiasm sounded real, Berkholdt's, I thought, a little forced.

Glancing at each of the armed men, I spoke in spite of my fear. "Listen, you two." I forced a smile. "In the business of the guns, you now enjoy what chess players call a stalemate."

Berkholdt scowled. MacDuff shrugged.

"I would suggest, therefore, that you both put away your weapon at once."

"Look, Berkholdt, she's right." MacDuff leaned back in his chair. "Neither of us can win. If one of us fires, so will the other. Probably we'd both end up dead."

"I'll put my gun on the table," MacDuff said, "if you'll put yours down -- at the same time."

There was a long moment of silence.

"And I will to make tea, my Sasha!" Emma Goldberg laughed nervously.

Berkholdt and MacDuff watched each other very closely, looking for signs. Keeping his gun pointed at MacDuff's chest, Berkholdt took a step forward and stood next to the table. Slowly, MacDuff brought his revolver from under the table. Each man held his gun a few inches above the wooden surface. Slowly, each man lowered his weapon. Finally, both guns clunked solidly down on the tabletop.

Emma got up and slid a fourth chair from against the wall over to the table.

"You will to sit, my Sasha?" she said.

Berkholdt sat down facing MacDuff. Miss Goldberg went to the stove and stirred life into the embers beneath the stovetop. She made tea, and then sat down again, across from me.

The four of us talked while the kettle warmed. Berkholdt and MacDuff sat and looked at each other and, I suppose, read each other's thoughts. Emma and I studied each other too. Emma leaned close to look at my hair, then at my eyes.

"Your hair, and your eyes, they speak of the continent which is dark -- no?"

I smiled.

"Ah! Miss Millicent, you are of my African sisters!"

"I am proud to say, Emma, that you are right."

I explained that my father had been a slave of both African and white origin, his father a white landowner. When England outlawed slavery in the 1840s, my father stole aboard an English ship in Savannah and escaped to Liverpool, where he met and married my English mother, and where I was born. My mother and I immigrated in 1875, upon my father's death.

"Miss Goldberg," I said, "you are very observant. Most people don't recognize my African features."

Most people don't know that MacDuff is one-quarter Cherokee Indian either. Most of the time, we both pass for white. Often, people think we are Italians.

"My father also was slave." Emma said sadly. "He was serf. There is little food all one winter. My father go off in woods, for to give to us his food. My father, he starve to death in woods!"

"Speak no more of this, my Emma," Berkholdt said, touching her arm. "It is very sad. And we have guests."

Emma looked at Berkholdt. "But who would think, that my Sasha, son of wealthy Russian businessman from Vilna, to the United States would come only few months ago, and to join anarchists whose business is to overthrow capitalists like his father?" She laughed.

"Hush now, Emma." Berkholdt grimaced.

"But of course, my Sasha." Emma said. She forced a smile. Then to me she said:

"Did you know Miss Anthony will to speak tomorrow evening at Brooklyn?"

"Yes! Will you be there, Emma?"

"Oh! But I cannot go."

Finally, MacDuff said, "Mr. Berkholdt, why did you and Miss Goldberg leave by Justice Schwab's back door when you saw us there last night?"

Berkholdt squirmed. He started to speak, but Emma interrupted.

She struck the table with her fist. "Some men in movement, other anarchists, they are stupid! They think my Sasha speak of too much violence. But kings of Capitalism never willingly will to abdicate their bloody thrones."

MacDuff raised his hand. "Please," he said. "My partner and I and I aren't here to talk politics."

"MacDuff is right, Emma," I said. "We are here to talk about the plot to kill Miss Anthony. Why, then, did you and your Sasha leave Justus Schwab's when we came in last night?"

Berkholdt took a deep breath, exhaled slowly. "I thought you, MacDuff, were of those men who think me dangerous to the Anarchist cause. In the dim light of Justus Schwab's, you look like a man who once threatened my life."

MacDuff gave Berkholdt a searching look. "As to our main reason for calling on you and Miss Goldberg, we want to know if either of you have heard anything about a plot to kill Susan B. Anthony?"

Berkholdt removed his glasses. Holding them up to the light, he inspected them for dust.

Berkholdt told us he had been walking one day recently in Little Italy, had come upon Gaetano's Saloon on Baxter Street, and went in to have a beer.

"I know the place," MacDuff said.

"Gaetano is a good friend of the people -- a good anarchist," Berkholdt said.

Berkholdt said he overheard two men talking at a table near his. One of them was Five Points Gang member Tony Daniello. The other was a man named Johnny Monk. Berkholdt said he heard Monk tell Daniello that somebody had hired a Five Points gang member to kill Miss Anthony."

"Johnny Monk also owns a saloon, doesn't he?" I said, addressing MacDuff.

"Yeah, over in Mulberry Bend." MacDuff said.

"Did Daniello name the man hired for the job?" MacDuff said to Berkholdt.

"No, Daniello did not give a name."

"Where can we find Daniello?"

"He used to stay in tenement on Canal Street," said Emma.

"Wait a minute," I said, looking at MacDuff. "I think I

have seen this Daniello. At a café in Little Italy. I was once in a play at a theater near there, and went to the café with friends after the last act. A well-known anarchist Leon Czolgosz gave a talk at the café that night, trying to raise funds. Czolgosz had hired Daniello to pass the hat."

"Ah! But I see my friend Gaetano yesterday." Berkholdt said. "He tells me Tony Daniello is now on way to Europe."

Berkholdt gazed at the ceiling. "But one never knows who is really on way to places."

MacDuff gave me a nod. We thanked the two anarchists for their hospitality and information.

"One more thing." MacDuff said. "Do either of you know if Daniello knows how to use a typewriter?"

They both laughed. They thought that Tony Daniello was too stupid.

MacDuff picked up his revolver and tucked it in his belt. We retraced our steps back through the garbage-strewn court, past the reeking privies, past the leaky hydrant, back onto Hester Street.

"MacDuff," I remarked after we had walked some distance, "you are unusually quiet tonight. Even for a Cherokee detective."

"Miss Goldberg's paramour, this Alexander Berkholdt. What do you think of him?" MacDuff said.

"You mean, do I believe his story about being an anarchist from Vilna?"

"Well, do you?"

I thought about it for a few moments. "I have reservations, MacDuff."

"What about his accent?"

"Russian, like Emma Goldberg's."

"I thought it sounded more like German."

We walked a few more blocks in silence.

"By the way, Millicent, what's Daniello look like?" MacDuff asked, as we strolled along Hester Street.

"Daniello, as I recall, is of average height, thin build with narrow shoulders, and is, I think, not more than twenty years old. When I last saw him, MacDuff, I thought he looked, well, unkempt."

"Not your Dapper Dan, as assassins go." MacDuff paused. "Okay, Millicent. Let's go and talk to Monk. Maybe he knows something."

"Maybe he could at least tell us where Daniello really is right now."

Chapter 7

It was half past four. Fog was drifting in from the East River. Hester Street looked even more dismal. Most of the pushcarts were gone. Shop owners had closed and locked their doors. Friday evening in Jew Town, the people were preparing for the Sabbath.

The sun shone dimly somewhere beyond the thickening fog. Here and there, a sudden breeze parted the gray curtain, and a ray of sunshine broke through the fog and crawled along the roof edge of the derelict buildings.

We continued down Hester to the Bowery, stopping briefly at a café for cabbage soup and bread.

"You must eat quickly," said the server who had beautiful hair. She went around shutting windows and scrubbing tabletops. Leaving the café, we walked south to a tenement house on Canal Street. It looked exactly like the tenements on Hester. The central court looked the same, too; same leaky hydrant next to a row of privies -- on all the streets the tenements were the same. This was the one we were looking for.

Two brown-eyed boys sat playing in the dirt next to the tenement stairs. MacDuff gave them each a dime, and the boys told us how to find Daniello's flat.

"Mr. Daniello, he lives way high up," the smaller boy said.

"Yeah, lady, way up at the top," said the taller one, and pointed to the stairs.

"We could show ya!" the smaller one said. "C'mon."

We followed the boys, the smaller one in the lead, up the stairs. They were standing waiting in the third floor hallway when MacDuff and I arrived, out of breath.

"Down there," the smaller boy pointed. "Last door on yer right."

"Thanks," MacDuff said, and handed each boy another dime.

The boys smiled at us, then at each other, then they clamored noisily back down the stairs in anticipation of bubble gum and licorice ticks.

MacDuff unbuttoned his coat, the quicker to reach his revolver. We walked to the door the boys had pointed out. MacDuff rapped on the worn center panel. We heard the shuffling of feet on the other side of the door. The door opened wide, revealing a large woman wearing too many clothes. Her hands were swollen and stained. The flat she lived in was her home and her factory. She was a cigar maker.

MacDuff showed the woman one of our printed cards. She gave it a glance, and then gave it back. Raising her hands, palms up, she grinned.

"No read'a the Englais," she said. "Italiano."

MacDuff looked at me. He knew I spoke better Italian. I introduced myself, also MacDuff. The woman's name was Maria. I told Maria we wanted to speak to Daniello.

"She says Daniello was a boarder but not anymore."

Stepping aside, the woman let us into her kitchen. Maria pointed at a pile of rags by the stove, and said it was where Daniello had slept. Then her tone changed, and she began saying unfavorable things about her ex-boarder.

"MacDuff, she says Daniello is no longer welcome in her flat."

For emphasis, Maria marched over and gave the pile of rags a kick, scattering the rags across the kitchen floor. Then she rattled off some more Italian, some of which were curse words. She glanced at the Mother Mary statue on a shelf next to the window and crossed herself. Maria spoke again. I summarized.

"It seems Daniello often came home drunk, and was always behind in his rent. She says he is now onboard a steamer bound for Europe. She says he is working his way across, as a stoker. Also, MacDuff, she says Daniello left owing her money."

"Ask her when he's coming back to the U.S.," MacDuff said.

I translated. The woman spoke, then spat on the floor.

"She says she fervently hopes Daniello never comes back."

Back down on Canal Street we stood next to a building. MacDuff spoke:

"The lady of the cigars said Daniello was on his way

to Europe. So did Berkholdt. We need more than their word," MacDuff said.

MacDuff glanced up and down the street. "Over there," he said.

We crossed over to the other side of Canal Street, and stopped and stood under a sign shaped like a shoe. Peering through the shop window, we saw the proprietor inside counting the day's receipts by lantern light.

"Trusting old soul," MacDuff said. He tapped on the window with his knuckle. The old man looked up. He frowned. MacDuff pressed a dollar flat against the glass. The proprietor unlocked the door, and opened it a crack. MacDuff slipped the greenback through the narrow opening. Then putting his mouth close to the door, MacDuff said:

"So where's Daniello these days?"

The shopkeeper grinned under his green visor.

"Daniello is on a steamship. They say he goes to Europe. Maybe he go there to kill King?" The shopkeeper laughed.

Such a rumor had been circulating at Justus Schwab's saloon. Anarchists planned to assassinate one of the few reigning kings left in Europe, possibly Tsar Nicholas.

"That's three, Millicent." MacDuff said, as we walked away from the shoe shop.

"I'm convinced," I said. "Daniello is on a steamship stoking coal."

MacDuff squinted, looked at me out of his blue eye.

"He's made damn sure people think so, Millicent."

And all of our contacts swore Daniello did not own a typewriter, nor could he use one if he did.

Chapter 8

It was now almost dark. We walked to the corner of Canal and the Bowery. Walking along the dreary street, we passed a drab building with a sign over the door that said Clinic. I pointed it out to MacDuff.

"MacDuff, I once saw Mabel Singer go in there. She had a young girl with her. The girl seemed reluctant to go in, but Mabel took her hand and practically hauled her inside."

"Say," MacDuff said. "Isn't it rumored that abortions are done there?"

"Yes, but it's never been proven."

"Also, MacDuff said, it is rumored that they sterilize people at that clinic. So I wonder just exactly why Mabel Singer dragged that girl inside."

"I assume she was giving some support to the young girl that she had with her. You know, MacDuff! The poor young thing was probably going to have an abortion. I have not heard that other rumor."

Just then a cab rattled slowly past. MacDuff hailed the cabbie. He pulled over, and we got in.

"Know a joint called Monk's?" MacDuff said to the cabbie.

"I know the place, but don't like going there." The cabbie heaved a sigh.

MacDuff reached in his pocket, pulled out two shiny Morgan's. The cabbie took the money, pulled away from the curb and rattled east on Canal towards the Mulberry Bend. Like Hester Street, the Bend was a marketplace. But the people were not Jewish. They were Italians, but like the Jews of Hester Street they were wretchedly poor.

The cabbie turned south on Mulberry, then came to a stop at the curb. MacDuff told the cabbie to wait, and paid him enough to make sure he would.

The entrance to Monk's Saloon was not actually on Mulberry Street. It was down an alley a few steps from where we got out. I followed MacDuff into the alley.

"Stay close, Millicent." MacDuff said. "It ain't called Blood Alley for nothing."

As we approached the entrance a huge brown rat scurried out of the shadows, and striking, I thought, a rather bold posture, stopped and stood in front of the swing doors. MacDuff swiped at the rat with his shoe. It moved unhurriedly back into the shadows.

"Well, here we are, Millicent," MacDuff said. "Monk's joint. Ain't it nice?"

"Oh, yes," I said. "Classy, indeed. They even have a doorman."

"Yeah, and if you think that was a big rat, wait till you see the two-legged ones inside."

"I suppose they have a hat check lady?" I peered over the top of the doors.

"Uh huh. Of course, instead of brushing your hat she picks your pocket. Okay, Millicent," MacDuff said. "Time to get serious."

I transferred my Iver Johnson from my shoulder bag to my shoulder holster. MacDuff removed his .38 from its holster and put it in his belt. He pushed open the doors, and we entered Monk's Saloon.

The gas was turned up in all the lamps, giving the place the garish look of a cheap waterfront dancehall. A woman standing at the bar watched us come in, the kind of woman the Mission workers call a painted lady.

Monk's joint did not have a maitre'd, so MacDuff led me to a table in back, and we sat down. The painted lady pushed herself away from the bar and sauntered over to our table, a bar towel draped over her arm.

"Yes?" she said, indifferently.

"Is Monk around?" MacDuff said.

"Buy the lady a drink," she pointed at me, "and maybe I'll tell ya."

"I'll have a beer," I said.

"Make mine coffee, straight up no chaser," MacDuff said.

The painted lady left. She came back and set a beer in front of me, a glass of something black, thick, and syrupy in front of MacDuff.

"No coffee, Mister. This, uh, soda will have to do."

She walked away. A man dressed all in black appeared at MacDuff's elbow.

"I'm Monk. What kin' I do for you?" he said, addressing MacDuff.

"Buy you a drink?" said MacDuff.

Monk shrugged. "Man walks in a saloon, says to the owner of the joint, 'kin I buy you a drink?'" Monk sat down between MacDuff and me. "Very funny. Watch me split a gut."

Monk looked me over. He smiled, nodded his head approvingly. I felt like a rack of lamb hanging in a Hester Street butcher shop.

MacDuff and Monk studied each other's attire. Both men were dressed all in black, down to their black suspenders. Other than that, however, Monk looked nothing at all like MacDuff. He was taller, and built like a barrel.

"I'm MacDuff. This is Millicent, my partner."

"I've heard'a ya. And yer partner," Monk said.

Monk did verify what Berkholdt told us about Daniello. He was, Monk said, on the way to Europe to kill a king. Then we got down to our main agenda.

"There's a rumor makin' the rounds, Monk. I wondered if you'd know, jist by chance you understand, if this here rumor was true?"

MacDuff not only had a working knowledge of the languages spoken in Lower Manhattan, he had also mastered the street gang vernacular spoken there. MacDuff could converse comfortably with anyone, actually. He was as comfortable conversing with college professors as he was when speaking with someone of Monk's ilk.

MacDuff lit a cigarette and blew smoke at the ceiling, where a Bowery artist had rendered a barroom version of Michelangelo's famous mural.

Monk shrugged. "What rumor could that be, Mr. MacDuff?"

"The one about the Suffrage lady, that somebody wants to kill her."

Monk looked toward the bar. He snapped his fingers. The painted lady came running, a drink in her hand. She set the drink on the table, gave Monk a broad smile and went away again. Monk stared at the drink.

"So happens, I myself have heard such a rumor, MacDuff." Monk gripped his thick glass until his knuckles were white. "But what does this rumor mean to you and this here lady?" Monk gave me a nod.

"Somebody hired us to make sure the rumor doesn't turn into the real McCoy," MacDuff said.

"Hard to stop an assassin, once he's loaded the gun," Monk smiled.

MacDuff and Monk sparred some more, then starting boxing in earnest. Finally, MacDuff leaned back in his chair, cocked his head sideways, shut his brown eye, and threatened to throw Monk a knockout punch.

"Say, Monk," MacDuff said. "An acquaintance of mine let it slip over beers one night, jist recently, about that there jewelry heist at the Dakota."

Monk tensed up. "The one what happened at that big apartment building up town? You mean that heist, MacDuff?"

"Yeah, Monk, that one. The Dakota, up on 72nd Street. Overlooks Central Park, don't it?"

"I might'a heard about it in one of the rags." Monk called the painted lady of the drinks back to the table. She set another drink in front of Monk, and scurried back to her station at the bar.

"Monk, this guy let fall on my ear that somebody separated a certain party living at the Dakota from twenty thousand dollars worth of sparklers. And the guy mentioned a name. Not the name of the lady who was robbed, Monk. No, he named the robber."

Monk gulped his drink, raised his empty glass above his

head. The woman with the face like a painter's palette came running. She set the drink on the table, ran back to the bar.

"You say this guy was drunk?" Monk squirmed.

"Yeah, but not too drunk to sign a statement."

"In front of our lawyer." I added.

I looked at Monk and smiled, as Eve must have when she handed Adam the apple.

"Millicent," MacDuff touched my arm. "you did put that there statement in our lock box at the bank, didn't ya?"

"Oh, yes, I most certainly did." I gave Monk a look. "Of course our lawyer has copies. To be turned over to the police, in case either of us should meet with an accident, or something?"

"Yep, Millicent, should either of us be so unfortunate."

Monk listened to our banter. I do not believe I have ever seen a man's face grow so red, so quickly.

"So, what do you think?" MacDuff looked at me. He glanced at his watch.

"Say, it's gettin' kinda late, Millicent." MacDuff pushed himself away from the table.

"Oh, my, yes it is, MacDuff." I faked a yawn.

We stood up.

"Listen, MacDuff." Monk put his hand on MacDuff's arm. "Sit down a minute. Okay?"

We sat down again.

"Bout that rumor, MacDuff. I think it could be true. Mind you, I said it might be."

"We want information, Monk. We want names and addresses. Real ones. Of people who jist might be involved in the plot to kill Susan B. Anthony."

I removed my journal and pen from my bag. I opened the journal, uncapped my Waterman. Monk talked, I wrote.

MacDuff was right about the rats inside Monk's place. They were big, and Monk was the biggest rat of all.

MacDuff knocked on my door a little before eight o'clock

next morning. He was grinning when I opened the door.

"Breakfast on Broadway, Millicent?"

"Certainly!"

He had on a clean black shirt, sported a fresh shave, and had pressed his trousers. I glanced at his feet.

"No time to shine the shoes, I see." He ignored my comment.

We walked to the little restaurant around the corner at Broadway and Third.

"Okay, Millicent," MacDuff said, patting his flat stomach, "time to go to work." We pushed soiled plates and silver aside, and opened our journals.

"Well, MacDuff, Monk supplied us with four names." I read from my notes. "Joey Sharpe, Jack Raven, Brian Donovan, and Ronald Eastman. We have addresses for all but Sharp. I suggest we take them in the order given to us, but save Joey Sharpe for last. We can locate his address later."

"It makes logical sense, Millicent. But being the Cherokee contrary that I am, I suggest we start with Ronald Eastman."

"Why Eastman?" I said.

"I was watching Monk's face as he gave us the names. When he got to Eastman, his face changed. He looked like he wished he hadn't given us Eastman."

Aboard the horse car, MacDuff gave me a biographical sketch of Ronald Eastman. In the old days, he was known by his professional name: Da Vinci. A member of the WHYOS in his youth, Eastman dropped out of the gang to take up the fine art of forgery. His specialty had been bonds and securities, rather than currency. He was the best in the business, a real artist. Thus his nickname, Da Vinci. Having made a considerable pile, Eastman, though not yet fifty, was now officially retired from the forgery racket. But he more than dabbled in politics, and was a favorite among Tammany Hall survivors.

Eastman lived uptown in a tall brownstone at 96th Street and Fifth Avenue, a very expensive neighborhood. Getting off the car at the corner, we walked half a block down Fifth to Eastman's three-story abode. MacDuff reached up to twist the ringer at the center of the door. His hand stopped in mid-air. Placing the tip of his index finger against the door, he gave it a gentle push. The door swung open a couple of inches.

We smelled a strong odor of gunpowder coming from inside the house. Ducking quickly away from the door, we drew our guns.

"Oh, oh, Millicent," MacDuff said under his breath. "Looks like somebody beat us to the interview."

"Damn! Damn! Bloody damn," I hissed.

We listened at the door. Then MacDuff pushed the door open further, and looked in. I peered over his shoulder. MacDuff turned and looked at me.

"I'm going in, he whispered."

"MacDuff -- be careful!" I said.

He went inside, leaving the door slightly ajar.

With a tight grip on my Iver Johnson, my finger on the trigger, I took a step in and craned my neck to see farther than the foyer. MacDuff moved silently through the foyer, and then crouching low, disappeared from view when he stole soundlessly into what was probably the parlor.

Now I could not see MacDuff at all. Nor could I hear him moving about, which, in itself, was not unusual. I stood and waited for what seemed an eternity, but was only a few minutes.

MacDuff poked his head out into the foyer. "Okay, Millicent," he said, "you might as well come in. There's no one here who can hurt us. Not anymore. Close the outside door, though, and, Millicent, throw the bolt."

MacDuff was right; there was no one there who could hurt us. But there was someone else in the room. MacDuff was sitting on a parlor chair, his revolver dangling loosely from his index finger. He was staring down at a man of about fifty, well-dressed, wavy hair graying at the temples. He lay in a heap on the floor in front of the hearth, dead of a gunshot wound to the head. It must have been a high caliber gun, there wasn't much left of Eastman's head.

I dropped down beside MacDuff and grabbed hold of his arm, and swallowed the lump in my throat. The odor of gunpowder filled the room. A cigarette end smoldered in an ashtray on the table next to the chair. MacDuff had already searched the premises before I came in, and found no one hiding under a bed or in a closet. Now he searched the body. The body was still warm.

MacDuff said he found the back door open when he searched that part of the house. He said he had seen a man running down the alley, saw him jump in a waiting coach and drive away.

There was something in the dead man's hand. MacDuff carefully unclamped the fingers. A wadded up ball of paper fell out onto the floor. MacDuff picked it up.

"What is that, MacDuff?" I said.

He straightened out the paper, and handed it to me. It was a brief hand-written note.

"Next time, it will be you, MacDuff, you and your little black helper."

"Obviously written by the killer," MacDuff. He crumpled it up and put it in Eastman's hand after killing him. How macabre!" I shivered.

We left Eastman's house and hurried to an Uptown branch of the U.S. Postal Service. Using a sheet of Postal Service stationery, we composed a letter to the NYC Police Department, telling exactly what we found, when and where we found it, and nothing more. I stuffed the letter, unsigned, in a Postal Service envelope, stuck a stamp on it and dropped it in the letter slot. It would reach police headquarters by the second post, around two o'clock.

"Millicent," MacDuff said, as we walked back to Fifth Avenue, "I need a cup of coffee." He made a face. "How 'bout you?"

I took his arm. "MacDuff, I thought you would never ask."

We found a small cafe nearby, where we sat and drank coffee and smoked and tried to make sense out of Ronald Eastman's murder.

"Why, MacDuff? Why was Eastman killed? And who killed him?"

MacDuff stirred his coffee with his index finger. He leaned back in his chair, closed both eyes and puffed smoke rings at the ceiling.

"Did Monk kill Eastman?" I said.

"What?"

To MacDuff, thinking was like watching a play at Palmer's Theater, except that he can step out of the audience, go up on stage and act as the director. He says he can change the props around in his mind, and adjust the lighting by turning the gas up or down, or by changing the location of the lamps. He can tell the actors where to stand or sit, even tell them what to say. He says a part of him can go up in the balcony, and looking over the railing see himself down in the main floor audience watching the play. I had interrupted the play he was watching. I leaned back and waited.

"…oh, yeah, Millicent." MacDuff looked at me. "It could have been Monk. But why?"

"Well, maybe Eastman was the only one Monk named who actually knew anything," I said, "and Monk was afraid Eastman would tell us something that might be, shall we say, embarrassing? Embarrassing not just for Monk, but perhaps to other people as well?"

"Yeah, that's one possibility. Or maybe Monk was thinking more about his own hide. If certain other people who also maybe live uptown, maybe some of those Tammany Hall politicians, found out Monk gave us names connected with the Anthony plot, then Monk could end up like Eastman. That is, if those other Uptown people have anything to do with the plot to kill Miss Anthony."

"So you think it could have been Monk who killed Eastman?"

MacDuff made a face. "No, I don't think Monk killed him. The man I saw running away from Eastman's house didn't look like Monk. He was taller, and built better.

"Of course, Monk might've hired somebody to do the job. Any new WHYO gang member would welcome the chance to prove himself. On the WHYO's list of services, it's called the Big One. The price: a hundred dollars."

"That is what a man's life is worth to one of those rats we saw at Monk's place. One hundred dollars?" I was appalled.

It was time to meet with Mrs. Beecher Hooker at her hotel.

Chapter 9

Inside the Fifth Avenue Hotel we crossed the lobby to the front desk, where stood a most proper stiff shirt, who gave us both what MacDuff calls the once-over. To say the least, MacDuff is no dandy. In fact, he loathes Victorian men's attire.

The clerk ran a practiced eye over MacDuff's apparel, making a mental note of deficits: no hat, no walking stick. Plain black jacket, black silk shirt, soft collar, no tie. Black trousers, black boots, unpolished, heels run down.

The clerk had been surveying my attire with his other eye, and finding no fault was now trying to ascertain whether I were an Italian, or heaven forbid, a negro.

"We're here to see Mrs. Beecher Hooker." MacDuff said, unfriendly-like.

"You say you wish to see Mrs. Isabella Beecher Hooker?" the clerk sniffed.

"That's what I said, dili," MacDuff held his nose.

I stifled a laugh. In Cherokee, dili means skunk. It is one of the few words I know in MacDuff's Native language.

"And you are?" The clerk gazed indifferently over MacDuff's head.

"My name's MacDuff, this is my partner Miss Davies."

The clerk glanced at a note on the desk.

"Oh, yes. I see that Mrs. Beecher Hooker is expecting you."

He snapped his fingers. A boy appeared out of nowhere and escorted us to the dining room, then to Belle's table. She was sitting alone, bent over black coffee and the morning edition of the *Times*. The boy cleared his throat. Belle looked up.

"Mr. MacDuff and Miss Millicent Davies," the boy said with a bow.

Belle removed her pince-nez. "Oh, yes!"

We sat down. The boy went away, and a waiter came to take our order. We dined while we discussed the case with Mrs. Beecher Hooker, who had already eaten.

"Since we saw you last, Belle," I said, "we have interviewed a number of persons who we felt could supply us with useful information. Two of those we interviewed are Emma Goldberg and her friend Alexander Berkholdt. Has Miss Anthony ever had dealings with either anarchist?"

Mrs. Beecher Hooker said that she and Miss Anthony had met Miss Goldberg and her friend at a Political Equality event. She said she and Miss Anthony had known Miss Goldberg for quite some time but had met Berkholdt only recently. They understood that Berkholdt had come to the U.S. only a few months ago. Mrs. Beecher Hooker said she and Miss Anthony held Miss Goldberg in high esteem because of her strong stand on Woman's Rights and Suffrage, but had not known Berkholdt long enough to form an opinion as to his character.

"Naturally," Belle said, "Miss Goldberg is more interested in the anarchist cause than the Suffrage movement, as we assume is the case with her friend Mr. Alexander Berkholdt."

Belle picked up her cup, sipped from it, set the cup back in the saucer. "In the realm of politics," she said, "Miss Anthony and I lean more toward the Socialist platform."

As we talked, for some reason Congressman Johnson came to mind. Mrs. Beecher Hooker said both she and Miss Anthony had met Johnson. He seemed, she said, to be a strong supporter of Suffrage.

Belle said that Johnson had given his support to a legislative proposal that would decriminalize the distribution of birth control information, which many Suffrage workers saw as beneficial to poor women who could not buy such information from a private physician. However, it was rumored that the pending bill would also legalize forced sterilization of women believed to be genetically defective. Most suffrage workers, Belle said, believed that forced sterilization was absolutely reprehensible. Both she and Miss Anthony were adamantly against it.

I told Mrs. Beecher Hooker that Miss Goldberg and Mr. Berkholdt mentioned two men who could provide us with information about the plot, and possibly give us names of likely suspects.

"And who are these men?"

"Tony Daniello and Johnny Monk."

Mrs. Beecher Hooker had not heard of either man, nor she thought, had Miss Anthony. This was no great surprise, since it was quite unlikely that either she or Miss Anthony counted any friends among NYC gang members.

We told Belle about our meeting with Johnny Monk, and that Monk indicated that a person or persons from the New York City underworld might have been hired to kill Miss Anthony. We told Belle about Eastman, whom we hoped might have provided us with valuable information. Then, of course, we explained why no such information was forthcoming.

"Apparently Mr. Eastman knew something," Belle said.

I spoke about the difficult and dangerous task MacDuff and I, and our agents, would face in the days ahead. And we talked about fees and expenses. MacDuff explained that we would have to keep Miss Anthony under surveillance twenty-four hours a day, and that we would need two deputy agents.

Once again Belle expressed the fear that one of our agents would speak to the press, or to the official police.

"If that happened," she said, "I am afraid Miss Anthony would make your job quite impossible. She might even change her itinerary without letting anyone know of the change, not even me."

MacDuff and I knew of one very good reason why the plot should be kept dark. Publicizing such a plot could cause someone else to formulate another similar plot. It could be especially dangerous if an actual attempt on Miss Anthony's life occurred. An attempt on Miss Anthony's life could lead to copycat attempts. They often occur when mentally unhinged individuals hear through the press about an attempted murder of a famous person. The unhinged individual then tries to kill either the same person, or some other famous person.

Again, we reassured her. We told her there is no chance our hired men would spill anything to the press, or the police.

"About expenses, Belle." MacDuff nodded to me.

MacDuff and I had talked this over, in detail, before arriving at the hotel. I told her that expenses, as MacDuff had said before, would be considerable. I said that we would also need a certain amount for unexpected expenses. For example, we would need out-of-pocket cash to pay for information that we could not obtain any other way.

"You mean you might have to bribe people?" Belle looked at the ceiling, and laughed.

These expenses, I told her, could total from three to four thousand dollars, not counting our fee of three thousand dollars each, over and above expenses.

Belle looked at MacDuff, then at me. There were tears in her eyes.

"I have already said money does not matter. Miss Millicent, Mr. MacDuff, whatever the cost, you and your agents must protect Miss Anthony. That is the only thing that matters."

We prepared to leave.

"Oh, just one more thing, Belle," I said. "By any chance did you tell anybody, anybody at all, that you had hired us to do some work for you?"

"Absolutely not!"

MacDuff said, "Millicent, never mind!"

"Belle, we were sure you hadn't. But I had to ask, because MacDuff recently had a little run-in with a four-wheeler."

"It was nothing, Belle!" MacDuff looked at me, and frowned.

I felt that Belle deserved to know the truth, and deserved to know just how dangerous was the case MacDuff and I had accepted.

"Well, not quite a run-in, but almost Belle, after receiving your wire we went out to interview some of our contacts. While we were out, someone in a coach tried to run over MacDuff."

MacDuff stared at me narrowly with his blue eye. Now I wished I hadn't opened my mouth about the incident.

Belle had just then picked up her cup to drink. She paused with it halfway to her lips. Setting the cup down, she placed her hand on MacDuff's arm.

"MacDuff, are you sure you and Millicent want to take on this case?"

MacDuff stared at me again out of his blue eye, and then abruptly changed the subject.

"About Miss Anthony's speaking schedule," MacDuff said. "Of all the stops on her schedule, which of them do you think will draw the biggest crowd?"

"Oh, the Spiritualist Camp in Western New York," Belle said without hesitation. "Miss Anthony is scheduled to speak there on Woman's Day."

"On August fifteen, according to the schedule," I said.
"Yes," Belle said. "The day has been set aside in Lily Dale this year especially to honor Woman's Suffrage and Political Equality. Miss Anthony shall be the special speaker of the day."

Belle leaned forward. "Mrs. Skidmore, one of the founders of Lily Dale, said to me last year that if Miss Anthony would only agree to speak on the Lily Dale platform, she would be guaranteed an audience of at least three thousand."

MacDuff drew a long breath. He exhaled slowly, shaking his head.

"Oh my, whatever is the matter?" Belle said.

MacDuff and I both knew that it would be a detective's nightmare. It meant that MacDuff and I, and two other agents would have to keep track of the movements of those three thousand people.

"Nothing is wrong, Belle," I lied.

Belle looked at MacDuff, then at me. "I am looking forward to going to the College of Psychic Studies this evening. Knowing that both of you will be there, I shall be confident that Miss Anthony will be safe."

MacDuff removed his watch from his vest pocket.

"It's half past two," he said. "Millicent and I have a lot to do before we go to Brooklyn tonight." He pushed himself away from the table. He looked at me.

"Now we shall need some expense money, Belle," I said."

Belle opened her purse, removed a thick envelope and set it on the table. The envelope was stuffed with bank notes of both large and small denomination. Shuffling through the notes, I quickly totaled them up. I looked at MacDuff. "Two thousand dollars," I whispered.

"That'll be fine, Belle," MacDuff said. I put the money in my bag

"Should you need more, wire me at my Connecticut home, Nook Farm," Belle said, and gave us each one of her calling cards.

MacDuff and I both sensed that Belle wanted to speak to me alone. MacDuff got up, abruptly, from the table, shook hands with Belle, and bade her goodbye. He told me that he was out of cigarettes, and would go and buy some at a shop in the lobby. I said I would meet him there in a few minutes. He strolled away from the table.

"Millicent," Belle said, after MacDuff left the dinning room, "I know I have given you and MacDuff a most dangerous assignment, and I would never forgive myself if something happened to either of you. I only pray that the two of you won't give up. Please, Millicent, promise me that you won't give up!"

Once more tears welled up in Belle's eyes.

"Belle," I said, touching her arm, "let me tell you something.

"In addition to his English last name, MacDuff has a Cherokee name as well, given to him by his Grandfather in a special ceremony. MacDuff's Cherokee name is Asgaya Waya, meaning Wolf Man. Belle, The Cherokee people say that once a Wolf discovers the scent of its prey, nothing can stop him -- nothing! That is, if he is a good Wolf. And, Belle," I said, "MacDuff is a very good Wolf."

Chapter 10

We left the Fifth Avenue Hotel and boarded a southbound car, our destination: the Bowery. We got off at Bowery Street and Park Row. Walking along the crowded sidewalk, we came upon a dive.

Taking MacDuff's arm, I went with him down the steps into the smoky basement saloon. A large man stood behind the bar. A foggy mirror, cracked here and there, ran along the wall behind him. On a shelf under the mirror stood a wooden trophy. On a brass plate it said The Champ, 1888.

"Hi Champ," MacDuff said, sliding onto a stool.

The stool I slid onto had one leg shorter than the others. It wobbled. The Champ glanced up.

"Hey, Wolf Man!" the Champ said, using MacDuff's Indian name.

The Champ came over, and leaning across the bar placed a ham-size fist on MacDuff's shoulder. The Champ's face bore many ugly scars, relics of his bare-knuckle boxing days. One of the scars curved around the right cheekbone for two inches. Half of his left eyebrow was missing. A lump of scar tissue covered the missing part. His left ear looked like a raw pork chop.

MacDuff introduced me. The Champ leered. MacDuff frowned.

"Uh, what'll you have, MacDuff?"

"Make it a beer, Champ," MacDuff hesitated, "for my partner." MacDuff nodded to me.

"Straight from the tap, Champ," I said. "No needled beer for me."

"The lady does know her beer," the champ said. "I don't sell any needled beer in my joint, lady'. Least not till after legal hours." The Champ laughed. It sounded like a pig snorting.

I chanced a sip of the beer that the Champ had pulled from the tap, and concluded that it probably would not cause blindness.

According to MacDuff, the Champ has another business. He is a sort of broker in the crime trade. He knows every hoodlum in New York, and their specialties. MacDuff says the Champ's nominal fees save people miles of legwork. Speaking of legs, if you should want somebody's legs broken the Champ will send you a man who specializes in that particular line. Need somebody for the big one. To bump off your bookie, or your heavily insured spouse? The Champ will find the right man for the job. "Bet on it," according to MacDuff.

"Champ," MacDuff said. "I need a couple of men."

The Champ grinned. "You need somebody to break a nose, maybe a leg, MacDuff?"

"No. I don't want somebody with knuckles for brains. I need a good-fella. No, two good-fellas."

The Champ drummed on the bar top with thick fingers.

"Ringo Norton comes to mind. How 'bout him, MacDuff?"

"Too young."

"Al Brady."

"Al would do."

"Oh, damn! I forgit. Al ain't available jist now, MacDuff, accounta he's doing a bit on Blackwell's Island. But, hey, I know a guy could get Al off the Island by tomorrow night. Cost ya, maybe twenty dollars."

"No," MacDuff said, "the guys I need have to be clean. No pending charges, not on the lam, nothing like that."

"That sure narrows the field, MacDuff. Let me think…."

The Champ rubbed his scarred face, propped his elbows on the bar top, clamped his teeth together and made a fist. He bit down on the first knuckle till it turned white. The Champ called this thinking.

Suddenly, the Champ slammed his fist down on the bar top. My beer stein jumped straight up. I caught it in time.

"Billy Bergin!" the Champ said.

MacDuff's face brightened. "Is Billy still around?"

"Yeah, MacDuff. Billy's fine right now, too, jist fine. He was doin' real well in the Green Goods dodge till one day a customer turned the tables. The mark shot Billy in the face. Billy's been lookin' real hard ever since for an easier way to make a buck."

I knew the Green Goods dodge to be a counterfeiting scheme.

"Shot in the face…" MacDuff closed his brown eye.

"Yeah, but you can't hardly tell, MacDuff. The Mark used a real little gun, a derringer. You know, one of them little guns gentlemen carry around to impress thur ladies." The Champ laughed. "The bullet went at an angle."

"Where can I find Billy now?"

"Up in the Tenderloin, is all I know," said the Champ.

I nudged MacDuff. "I know Billy and I know his mother, too," I said. "My mother and I lived near them when we first came here from England. And I know Billy from the Theater too. He once played himself in a Lower Broadway piece about the Green Goods business. I played Billy's 'moll.'"

MacDuff reached across the bar and slipped some banknotes into the Champ's shirt pocket.

"Thanks, Champ," MacDuff said.

The Champ smiled, and we left.

Chapter 11

Billy Bergin's mother owned a neighborhood café at 26th Street near 6th Avenue, in the heart of the Tenderloin. Some of the nicer Manhattan saloons operate there. After legal hours, some of the saloons turn into Black and Tan clubs, where white and Negro patrons mix. A few saloons turn into high-class bordellos. It is no secret. We took a Fifth Avenue car, got off at 26th Street, and walked from the corner to the café.

I led the way inside. Mrs. Bergin looked up from the counter.

"Will wonders never cease!"

Mrs. Bergin is a large, light-skinned black woman with thick arms and straightened hair.

"It is good to see you, Momma!" I said.

"Millie, Millie!" We leaned across the counter, and kissed. "And who is this man?" Mrs. Bergin flashed MacDuff a big warm smile.

"His name is MacDuff, Momma. He's a private detective -- I'm his partner, Momma! He and I are on a case." I took MacDuff's arm. "We want to see Billy."

"What for?" Momma Bergin's eyes narrowed.

"Nothing bad, Momma. No. No," I assured her. "MacDuff has a job for Billy."

"Exactly what kind of job, Millie?" Momma leaned against the counter. She shot a glance at MacDuff.

"Honest work, Mrs. Bergin," MacDuff said.

Momma Bergin turned to me, and talked about MacDuff as though he weren't there.

"He doesn't look like no white boy, but he's not black either. Whatever he is, Millicent, is he an Honest John, or just look like one, and what's wrong with his eyes? They look funny."

"You're right, Momma, MacDuff is not quite white, and not black either. He's part Indian. His eyes, well, they don't match. He was born that way, Momma. And he is a real Honest John, not a phony.

Momma Bergin eyed MacDuff again. "Where did you grow up?"

"Lower East Side."

"I mean, before you came to New York?"

"The Cherokee Nation East, Mrs. Bergin. North Carolina. In the mountains."

"I know where it is. One of my aunts married an Indian man from there. What I want to know, is what did they call you back there in North Carolina, MacDuff. I mean what did the white folks call you?"

"They called me a redskin nigger, Mrs. Bergin."

Momma Bergin laughed till she shook. Leaning across the counter, she gave MacDuff one of her famous Momma Bergin bear hugs.

"Welcome to the Tenderloin, MacDuff!" she said.
Releasing MacDuff, she pointed toward the back of the café with her chin.

At a table next to the rear door, a pair of fine brown hands held up a newspaper. Smoke curled up from behind the newspaper. MacDuff and I walked over and stood next to the table. The brown hands folded the newspaper slowly in half, then deftly folded it in half once more, revealing a light brown face. Billy smiled, and set his cigar in the ashtray.

"It's been a long time, MacDuff, Millicent." Billy nodded at two empty chairs across the table from him.

MacDuff and I sat down.

MacDuff and Billy had known each other since they were kids. Both had been newsboys. On one occasion, they shared a jail cell at the Tombs. Both of them ended up, eventually, serving time on Blackwell's Island.

"So, Billy," MacDuff said after the small talk, "the Champ says you're tired of having holes shot in your face. He says you're ready to consider a different kind of stall."

"The Champ's right," Billy said. "You're still in the private detective business, MacDuff?"

"Yeah. Listen, Billy, Millicent and I are on a real important case, and we need help. We need you, and one other good fella who'll work with you. You'll be deputy agents, working under my license. We'll pay you ten Morgan's a day, your helper three. You hire him, you supervise him. All expenses paid. Food, cab fare, train fare, hotels, clothes."

"Sounds good. Too good. What's the catch, MacDuff?"

"You and the man you'll be boss over would have to stay loyal to me and Millicent. I mean a hundred per-cent. And you both have to be ready to take a fall, if it comes to that."

"Ten Morgan's a day, that's big money for honest work." Billy smiled. He reached up and touched the scar below his right eye. The eye twitched. The smile faded.

"Yeah, Billy." MacDuff read his thoughts. "Somebody could turn the tables on you again."

Billy picked up his cigar from the ashtray. His eye stopped twitching.

"Okay, MacDuff, what's the deal?" Billy said.

"Billy, somebody plans to kill the suffrage lady Susan B. Anthony. Millicent and I have been hired to stop him."

Billy whistled. "The plot's for real, MacDuff?"

"It's real, Billy."

MacDuff and I explained the case in detail. Billy listened. He smoked another cigar. MacDuff and I waited.

Finally, MacDuff said, "Well, Billy?"

Billy looked at MacDuff, then at me. "When do I start?" He said.

"Right now," I said.

Excitement showed on Billy's face. "I already have that other good fella in mind," He said.

"Bring the man around to see us tomorrow afternoon," MacDuff said. "Expect a wire, here, in the morning that'll say where and what time."

"I'll watch for the Western Union boy, MacDuff."

"Now, Billy, listen close."

MacDuff and I told Billy about our meeting with Johnny Monk. As it turned out, Billy knew Monk. And it came as no surprise that Billy also knew all the suspects on the list of names Monk had given us. Billy had once worked among the same circle of gangsters. He described each suspect in surprising detail.

MacDuff asked whether Billy thought any of the men on the list would commit murder. Billy folded his arms across his chest, unfolded them. "Raven more likely than then the rest, but any of them, I think, if the money was right."

MacDuff looked at his watch. "Millicent and I have a lot to do before this day is done. Tell us more about these guys next time we meet, Billy."

"Then it's a deal?" Billy said.
MacDuff and I exchanged looks. "Yeah, Billy, it's a deal." We shook hands on it.

"Hey, I'm a private eye," exclaimed Billy. "Just like one of those Pinkerton guys!"

"Billy," I said, "we're better than that Pinkerton bunch! And don't you forget it."

Billy walked with us to the door.

"Then we'll meet again tomorrow afternoon?" he said.

"That's the plan right now," MacDuff said, then paused. "But in the private detective business, you have to be ready to change your plans. MacDuff snapped his fingers, "that fast! So be ready to jump on a train with us any time of the day or night, Billy." We shook hands again.

On our way back downtown we passed Brentano's Literary Emporium at 16th Street. It made me think of when I first met MacDuff. This part Indian man who, at times, talked like a common thief, was an expert on classical literature. Naturally I wondered where he had gone to college.

"Brentano's." he had said.

"Oh," I remember saying, "it sounds Italian." I was quite naïve, I know. "In Rome?"

"Nah," he said. "Broadway and 16th. Brentano's Literary Emporium"

It was at Brentano's that MacDuff discovered Shakespeare and Keats, Plato and Aristotle, Emerson and William James. For eight winters, from age eight to sixteen, MacDuff picked Brentano's backdoor lock each night, after closing, and read till dawn by candlelight.

A crowd of people carrying signs stopped our car near the Cooper Union. Some of the signs said, "Social Darwinists Not Welcome at NYU!" Another one said, "Eugenics Means Racism!" NYU students, mostly, of both sexes, from the nearby campus out in large numbers to protest a lecture by Herbert Spencer, father of Social Darwinism.

Another group of marchers, a smaller all-male group composed mostly of older men, also carried signs, and their signs made me angry! One sign said, "Immigrants! Criminals! Morons! Weed Out the Unfit!" Another said, "No Charity for Defectives!" Yet another sign read, "Sterilization - Birth Control that Works!" The sign that caught my attention most, and made me cringe, was the one that said, "When Stupid Women Win the Vote, Human Waste will Govern Rational Men."

We recognized some of the protesters.

"Say," MacDuff quipped, "isn't that the mother of birth control? I mean Mabel Singer."

"I know who you mean, MacDuff! But the mother of birth control. Now, really!"

"Relax, Millicent, I know people say she does good work. Which side is she marching with?"

"With the college students, of course! Did you know Mrs. Singer has more than once, even gone to jail for her cause?"

She was trudging along in the midst of the protesters, a tall young woman with blond hair. A man marching along beside her might have been Mrs. Singer's husband James Singer. He was a strong advocate of Mrs. Singer's cause, and he, too, had gone to jail once for distributing his wife's birth control pamphlets.

I did not say so to MacDuff, but I did have some reservations regarding Mrs. Singer. One of the editing staff at the *New York Sun*, a close friend of mine, in fact, who had once been a strong advocate of Mrs. Singer's Family planning organization, shared with me a disturbing bit of news about Mrs. Singer. According to my friend, Mabel Singer was purported to have once said, "The poor, who are nearly all immigrants, bring with them to our shores defective traits which doom them to failure. They are, essentially, human weeds."

    Surely my friend at *the Sun* was mistaken.

Chapter 12

We hired a cab from the hack line across from our building, and rode to Brooklyn. We got out of the cab in front of the college, and sent the cabbie down the street to wait.

The College of Psychic Studies did not look like a college. No climbing ivy, no mullioned windows. It was a brownstone row house with half a dozen stone steps rising to a stoop. At the top of the stoop was a sturdy oak door. MacDuff twisted the big brass key in the middle of the door. A bell sounded. The door swung open. A tall woman in black with lace at her throat looked first at me, then at MacDuff.

"Good evening, dear," she said looking at me. She looked at MacDuff as though he weren't there.

"Hello," I said, waving my reporter's notebook. "We are here for the lecture."

"Well, you are quite early. The program will begin at eight o'clock." She turned to look at the grandfather clock which stood at the other end of the foyer. "It is now just a few minutes past seven."

"We shall not mind waiting," I smiled. "My name is Miss Jennings, of the *Philadelphia News*, and this is my associate Mr. McHenry." I gave her one of my fake cards. "We have been sent by our editor to cover Miss Anthony's speech. We should like to reserve our chairs now, if that will not inconvenience you?"

The woman glanced once more at the clock, and while her head was turned, MacDuff took my arm and pulled me inside the foyer.

"Well. Uh. It is, as I said, rather early, you see. But…"

The tall lady was flustered, but quickly regained her composure. She said, "My name is Miss Billings. That's with two ells. Do follow me, Miss Jennings."

"Ah, two ells." I opened my reporter's notebook and scribbled something.

Miss Billings led us past the grandfather clock, then through a set of pocket doors into the lecture hall. Six rows of straight back wooden chairs, two chairs in each row, stood on either side of a center aisle. Twenty-four chairs in all.

A lectern stood at the front of the room. An exit door, directly behind the lectern, led out to an alley. There were no other doors. There was a tall narrow window to the right of the door.

Miss Billings stood by the open pocket doors watching us look the place over, then excused herself to answer the doorbell. MacDuff walked quickly to the exit door to see if it was locked. It was. So was the window.

We chose aisle seats across from each other in the back row, and could survey the entire hall from there.

"MacDuff, this really is not a good place to make an assassination attempt," I said.

"Maybe not, Millicent…" MacDuff's voice trailed off.

I heard the bell ring again at the main entrance door. MacDuff and I sat down. MacDuff pretended to study his program, I fanned myself with mine. Miss Billings showed three people into the hall, then rushed to usher in more people. MacDuff and I scrutinized each person who entered. Soon the doorbell stopped ringing. The hall was now full.

No one there looked like an assassin.

Miss Billings came into the hall, closing the doors behind her. She strode quickly to the front of the room and stood behind the lectern.

"Good evening, ladies," she paused. "And, uh, gentlemen." There was a nervous catch in her voice. "Welcome to the College of Psychic Studies." Miss Billings coughed, cleared her throat, and then stepped from behind the lectern.

The pocket doors slid open. A small elderly woman, slender, conservatively dressed, walked quietly into the hall. I recognized immediately that famous profile. The well-defined cheekbones, the iron gray hair pulled into a bun at the back of the head, the head held high. The poise, the confidence, the effect was unmistakable. A hush fell on the hall. Miss Susan B. Anthony walked quickly to one of the chairs behind the lectern, and sat down. The faintest of smiles showed on her un-rouged lips.

Then Belle came in. Leaning her considerable weight on her stout cane, she walked slowly, stiffly down the aisle past the lectern, and sat down next to Miss Anthony.

Miss Billings stepped up to the lectern. She made the formal introductions, starting with Belle who stood and smiled brightly. Then Miss Billings introduced Miss Anthony.

"And now, on behalf of the College of Psychic Studies, I am ever so pleased and proud to introduce our speaker for the evening, Miss Susan B. Anthony!"

Miss Billings sat behind the lectern next to Belle.

Miss Anthony spoke more than an hour. Everyone there was mesmerized, not so much by the speech as by the speaker's persona. The great lady exuded confidence, sincerity, and intelligence.

Suddenly MacDuff leaned toward me across the aisle.

"The window, Millicent!" he hissed.

Glancing quickly at the narrow window at the back of the room, I saw a man's face looking in. MacDuff jumped up and raced down the aisle. Holding his revolver close against his midsection so no one would see it, he stood between the window and Miss Anthony. Running down the aisle behind MacDuff, my Iver Johnson hidden in the folds of my skirts, I stopped and stood next to him. The person outside in the alley (I'm sure it was a man) held a gun pointed at MacDuff's chest! I stifled a scream! I saw Miss Anthony stiffen and catch her breath. MacDuff smashed the window with his elbow. Shards of broken glass flew out into the alley; the man outside the window vanished.

Miss Anthony threw both hands to her face, but she made no sound. Belle struggled to her feet and limped to Miss Anthony's side.

The window was too narrow to climb through, so MacDuff ran to the locked door. He took three steps back. He lunged at the door with his shoulder, but the door held fast. He tried a second time; still, the door held. On the third try, the lock gave, screws and hinges tore loose, and the door with part of the frame still attached crashed into the alley behind the hall. MacDuff dashed out through the opening.

I turned and faced the people in the room.

"Stay here!" I yelled. "It is the only safe place!" All of the people ran to the corner of the room that was farthest from the shattered window and broken-down door.

Knowing Belle's driver John would be waiting out front with the coach, Miss Anthony and Belle went out through the pocket doors into the lobby, then out the main door. I followed. I stood on the stoop in the shadows, watching and listening.

Belle's driver, John, stood waiting next to the coach, his hand on the coach door. Miss Anthony and Belle went down the steps and stopped next to John.

Naturally, Belle had known all along that MacDuff and I had been in the audience, but I knew she would say nothing to Miss Anthony. With so many exciting things happening at once, we hoped Miss Anthony would not remember what MacDuff and I looked like.

"John," Belle said, speaking rapidly, "I want you to whisk Miss Anthony to Grand Central Station with the greatest possible haste!"

"As you say!"

"And I do not want you to leave her side until you see her safely aboard the next train to Poughkeepsie. Do you understand, John?"

"Absolutely!"

"You needn't return for me. I shall hire a cab, and shall meet you at the Fifth Avenue Hotel in the morning for breakfast. Then we must catch the morning train to Nook Farm."

Belle gave Miss Anthony a hug, and stepped back with her cane. John helped Miss Anthony into the coach, jumped up on the coachman's seat and drove away.

A few minutes later MacDuff showed up at the front of the building. I walked down the steps and joined him and Belle.

"Belle! Where is Miss Anthony?" MacDuff was angry.

"On her way to Grand Central Station, to catch the train to Poughkeepsie," Belle said. "John will stay with her until she is safely aboard. Those were my strict orders."

"I wish you'd told John to go with her. Miss Anthony won't be safe alone on that train!"

"Who was the man whose face we saw in the window, MacDuff," I said, "and where did he go?"

"I don't know, Millicent. Damn! When I went out in the alley I saw him jump in a coach at the corner and drive off. For all I know, he might've been one of the men from our suspect list."

"Yes, and MacDuff!"

"Yeah, I know." MacDuff slammed his fist into his palm. "And he might be at this minute climbing aboard a train with the woman we're supposed to protect!"

"Oh, I pray to God he is not on that train." Belle wrung her hands.

Miss Billings now joined us in front of the building. MacDuff apologized for destroying the rear door of the lecture hall. He convinced Miss Billings that he had been trying to protect us all from being robbed at gunpoint by the man at the window. MacDuff and I hoped that the police would like the story too. MacDuff gave Miss Billings money to pay for damages. Now we had to get away before the police arrived on the scene.

MacDuff whistled for our cab. The cabbie drove up and stopped at the curb. No, he had not seen the man at the window, had not seen him run, or drive away from the scene.

By now some of the people inside began to trickle out.

"C'mon," MacDuff said to Belle. "Millicent and I will drive you to your hotel."

We helped Belle into our cab, and got in with her. Just as I jumped in, I glanced up over the cab roof. High in a treetop across the street I saw an owl silhouetted against the moon. How odd, I thought, to see an owl in Brooklyn.

We pulled up and stopped in front of Belle's hotel, and walked her inside.

"Thank you so much, both of you," Belle said tearfully. "Now I know you shall keep my friend safe."

"Bet on it," MacDuff said.

"Oh, Miss Millicent," Belle said, "I meant to give this to you before." Reaching into her bag, she took out a folded sheet of paper.

"Miss Anthony abhors hotels," Belle said. "This is a list of the names and addresses of the people with whom she stays when on a speaking tour in New York State." Belle handed the list to me.

"Is there any chance the would-be assassin might have got hold of the same information?" MacDuff asked.

"I do believe it was once included in a news article, but that was ever so long ago."

"C'mon, Millicent! We've barely enough time to catch the midnight train to Poughkeepsie. And we still have to stop and pick up Billy Bergin."

I followed MacDuff back out to the cab.

"Washington Square, driver, and hurry!" MacDuff shouted as we jumped in.

Chapter 13

On our way to Washington Square, MacDuff lectured me incessantly upon the extreme danger involved in the case we were now on. Mostly, I ignored him.

Arriving at our building, MacDuff ordered the driver to wait. We ran to the entrance, unlocked the door and went quickly inside. I removed my latchkey from my bag. MacDuff put his hand on my arm.

"Millicent?"

"MacDuff?" I said, my key in my hand.

"What if there's a development, I mean here in the City?" he said. "And you're not here to take care of it?"

"Save your breath, MacDuff," I said, unlocking my door.

"Then there's no talking you out of it. You are going with me?"

"Just you try and stop me, MacDuff!"

He shook his head, turned and started up the stairs, then stopped.

"Okay, Millicent. Pack one grip," he said. "Only one grip."

"Surely I will need two!"

"One, Millicent, and make sure it'll fit under a train seat. And your shoulder bag. Yes you can take that along, but nothing else."

"Oh blast!" I said, using my English mother's favorite swear word.

My mother who had died two years ago, what a woman she had been. An aristocratic lady of impeccable antecedents, she had pushed my pram down London daylight streets, proud, her head held high, my dark-skinned father at her side, daring anyone to say anything.

I woke from my reverie when MacDuff said, "Look, Millicent, if Nellie Bly traveled round the whole damn world carrying a single grip, you oughta be able to go across New York State, and back, with only one grip."

MacDuff was right about Nellie Bly, and her famous single

grip. I chose an old style carpetbag. Flexible, easy to handle. I hauled the old thing out of the closet, shook the dust from it. Then I opened Nellie Bly's Around the World in Seventy-Two Days, and duplicated as much as possible the list of clothing and personal items Nellie Bly swore was all she had with her on her amazing round-the- world tour.

Like Nellie, I packed only two basic outfits, and the bare minimum of personal items. I stowed my revolver in my shoulder bag, the holster in my grip. I don't think Nellie carried a revolver. Just as I finished packing, there was a knock. I yelled come in. MacDuff smiled when he opened the door and found me holding one piece of luggage in my hand, and my bag slung over my shoulder.

"Nellie Bly would be proud, Millicent!"

"Oh, hush, MacDuff!"

I had stuffed into my shoulder bag Nellie Bly's famous book, also a copy of the *New York Sun* article Nellie had written after interviewing Miss Anthony at her Rochester, New York, home. After reading it, I felt I knew Miss Anthony well.

Before leaving our building, I pinned a note to the landlady's door, begging her to "please take good care of MacDuff's cat Shadow, and my canary La Scala," while we were away. It was not the first time I had imposed on her.

The last train to Poughkeepsie would leave in forty-five minutes. All the way to the Tenderloin to pick up Billy, we worried that he would not be at the café. And we worried about whether we were being followed.

MacDuff pounded on the locked café door. A thin strip of yellow light showed briefly when an inside door at the back of the place opened, then closed. A shadow moved through the café. The front door opened.

"MacDuff, Millicent, c'mon in."

We went inside, and Billy shut and relocked the door.

"What brings you here this hour of the night?" Billy said.

"Change of plans, Billy," MacDuff said. "We have to go to Grand Central Station, I mean right now!"

By now, I was frantic. "There is a cab waiting outside, Billy," I said. "Please hurry! We'll explain on the way."

"Just a minute," Billy said. "There's someone in back you have to meet, a good fella. Decided to bring him here tonight, just in case. I remembered what you said, MacDuff." Billy snapped his fingers. "Hope you'll think he's okay for the job."

We followed Billy through the darkened café, then into a windowless back room. A man stood next to a table. There was an oil lamp on the table, turned down low. I turned the flame higher. The man standing next to the table was of medium height, slender, clean-shaven with a ruddy face and light blue eyes. His dark brown hair was neatly trimmed. A quick glance at his hands told me he had never known hard work.

"This is George Dixon," Billy said. "Dixon, Art MacDuff and Millicent Davies."

MacDuff nodded. I said hello.

"Billy, we need to talk to you alone," MacDuff said.

MacDuff, Billy, and I stepped out of the room.

"We have to catch that midnight train, Billy," MacDuff said. "Miss Anthony's life probably depends on it. If you think this guy's okay, then Millicent and I will interview him on the way to Grand Central. How about it, Billy, is he okay?"

"He's okay, MacDuff. Bet on it."

"Then, let's go."

"I better let Momma know."

"There's no time, Billy. Wire her from Poughkeepsie."

The four of us piled into the cab.

"Grand Central Station, cabbie, and go like hell!" MacDuff yelled.

It was about half a mile from the café to Grand Central, at 42nd Street and Park Avenue. The hour was late, no traffic to fight. If we were lucky, we would arrive in time.

After telling Billy what happened in Brooklyn, MacDuff and I grilled Dixon all the way to the station. Dixon claimed to be a graduate of Inspector Byrne's third-degree school. He said Byrne's underlings took turns beating him with a rubber hose and choking him with his own necktie.

"Did you crack?" MacDuff gave him his one-eyed stare, the blue-eyed one.

"No!"

"It's true, MacDuff," Billy said. "I was in the same cell block that night."

"Okay, Dixon," MacDuff said. "Let's say, for now you're in."

"Say, Mr. MacDuff," Dixon said. "Ain't I seen you somewheres before?"

MacDuff and I had looked closely at Dixon's face before we left the café. There were some scars. MacDuff asked Dixon whether he boxed. Dixon nodded affirmatively. He looked at MacDuff in the darkness of the coach.

"Yeah, I boxed some. Hey, MacDuff! That's where I seen you. At Hoffmeister's Gym. You're the guy what knocked me out! We was sparrin' and you got lucky with a left jab."

"It was a left jab alright." MacDuff grinned. "But I didn't get lucky, you left yourself wide open."

Dixon rubbed his jaw. "I ain't never been hit so hard by a left jab. It'll be a pleasure workin' fer you, MacDuff!"

When we boarded the train, we had the car to ourselves. We talked business. First thing we accomplished was to put Billy officially in charge of his mob of two, as MacDuff phrased it. Then we gave Billy two hundred dollars for his and Dixon's expenses.

"If this runs out, Billy, let us know," I said.

Billy nodded.

MacDuff explained the details of the operation. I gave them each a copy of Miss Anthony's schedule and a copy of the list of names and addresses of the people with whom she would stay at each city on her tour.

"As soon as we arrive in Poughkeepsie," MacDuff looked at Billy, "you and Dixon rent a carriage and go to where Miss Anthony's staying according to the list. She should be there already. That's the first thing you'll do at each city where she stops to do a speech, shadow her from the depot to where she'll stay while in that city. You'll have to hire a carriage as soon as you detrain. There's always a bunch of liverymen with carriages waiting outside the depot.

"Billy, you and Dixon will have to watch Miss Anthony every minute. And don't let her see you! If she finds out she's being shadowed, she'll make our work a lot harder."

"This isn't going to be easy, is it MacDuff?" Billy said, "Especially with her being so uncooperative."

"You're right. Miss Anthony's damned smart, and full of surprises. But she's only trying to protect what she believes in, Billy."

"Yeah, I know, MacDuff. I've got a lot of respect for the lady."

"She will arrive at Poughkeepsie tonight long before us," I said.

"This time," MacDuff said, "we'll just have to guess she's where the list says she'll be.

"So, your job, yours and Dixon's, Billy, will mostly be to shadow Miss Anthony everywhere she goes, everywhere. During the night, you'll work in shifts. One of you has to be awake watching the place where she'll stay the night, and you'll have to shadow her wherever she goes during the day. It'll be a round-the-clock business."

"Millicent and I'll go early to the places Miss Anthony goes to speak, to see what kind of security problems we'll be up against. And we'll look for places an assassin could hide. We'll study the neighborhood, and the streets she'll travel on. One or both of us will meet up with you and Dixon, to let you know what our investigation reveals. For example, we'll tell you if we think there's any place along the route you need to pay special attention to."

"Okay, MacDuff," Billy said. "Now how about when Miss Anthony's inside the hall doing her speech?"

"Once Miss Anthony goes into the hall, Millicent and I'll go inside too. Billy, you and Dixon will be outside making sure nobody tries to sneak in a front or back exit, to take a shot at her."

Billy smiled. "I understand, MacDuff. It's like knocking off a bank. Same thing, really. You and Millicent are taking care of business inside. Dixon and I are outside making sure no one goes in and interferes with the business being transacted with the tellers."

We laughed at Billy's apt metaphor.

"Be on the lookout for packages, too," I said. "Bombs."

"Damn," Dixon said in an undertone.

"She didn't say a bomb is likely," MacDuff added. "It's not. The would-be assassin wouldn't want to make that much noise. But do like Millicent said, watch out for packages."

"This is how we'll handle things when we're traveling," I said.

"Listen to her, you two. Listen carefully." MacDuff said.

"When Miss Anthony boards a train," I began, "naturally all four of us will climb on board too. MacDuff and I will be on the same car as Miss Anthony. Billy, you and Dixon will be in the one behind Miss Anthony's car. Once we're underway you two will take turns walking the length of the train, and you'll check out all the passengers in each car. Observe the train staff too, the porters, the dining car waiters, and the conductor.

"Although MacDuff and I will be in the same car with Miss Anthony, most of the time we'll take separate seats so we will have a better chance to watch Miss Anthony without her seeing us. We'll bribe the conductor, if we have to, in order to get the best seats."

"After while, won't Miss Anthony start to notice us?" Billy said.

"Billy, you and Dixon will have to buy clothes anyway, since we didn't give you a chance to pack a grip."

"I wondered about that," Billy said.

"We gave you enough expense money to buy changes of clothes in every town we stop in." I said.

MacDuff picked it up from there. "Lucky for you and Dixon, Miss Anthony has never laid eyes on you two. She probably saw Millicent and me in Brooklyn earlier tonight. We hope she won't remember us but she might. Anyhow, we'll all have to change how we look, probably every day."

MacDuff turned to me. "Millicent?"

"These items will help, Billy." I pulled my carpetbag from under the seat, and opened it. Reaching inside, I lifted out the wide assortment of professional theatrical props and makeup I brought along for the job. I took out what I thought MacDuff and I would need, and then divided the rest of the goods between Billy and Dixon. Billy recognized the things from his stage experience.

"Everything you need is there," I said. "Mustaches and beards, creams to lighten the skin or make it darker, shoe lifts to make you taller, even cotton batting to tuck in your mouth to change how your face looks."

"Excellent, Millicent!" Billy grinned.

"Jist like that there English gent, Sherlock Holmes," Dixon laughed.

"Dixon, Billy has been on the stage so allow him to help you with your makeup," I said.

Dixon nodded.

"Soon after we arrive in a city, after you and Dixon follow Miss Anthony to where she'll be staying," MacDuff said, "we'll locate you as soon as possible and provide you with the name and address of our hotel.

"If you need to contact us, and we're not at our hotel, look for us wherever Miss Anthony will do her speech. But make sure one of you stays on Miss Anthony's tail every minute! It's important, by the way, that we meet once a day, at least, so we can share information and go over our plans."

MacDuff paused. "One more thing, are you both armed?"

"Got you covered, there," Billy laughed. "Will this do?"

He unbuttoned his coat and showed us the large revolver stuffed in a holster under his left arm. MacDuff smiled approvingly.

"And this?"

Billy's hand went inside his coat again. It came back out holding a policeman's blackjack. He struck the palm of his other hand with the ugly weapon, making a loud 'thwack!'

"Okay," MacDuff laughed. "Where's your brass knuckles?"

"Left the knuckles home," Billy grinned.

He pulled up his pant cuff and showed us a leather pouch strapped to his leg just below the knee. Protruding from the pouch was the pearl handled grip of a double-barrel derringer.

MacDuff shook his head. "How 'bout you, Dixon?"

Dixon, grinning proudly, showed us two revolvers and one very large ugly knife.

Chapter 14

Arriving in Poughkeepsie, we looked at the list. Miss Anthony would stay with a Mrs. Ballenger, 432 Park Lane Blvd. MacDuff and I accompanied Billy to the livery next to the station, where Billy hired a coach. Using directions provided by the liveryman, he and Dixon would easily find the Ballenger residence. MacDuff and I drove our hired coach to a nearby hotel, the Newby, and booked side-by-side second floor rooms.

A knock on my door woke me in the morning. Daylight poked feebly in my window at the edge of the curtains. I got up, threw on my robe. "It's too bloody early," I said to nobody at all. I opened the door and MacDuff came in with a morning newspaper tucked under his arm. I went to the window, threw the curtains wide, and sat down in the armchair next to the window. MacDuff plopped down in the chair by the hearth, set the newspaper on the floor by his feet, and stretched his legs. MacDuff's legs were disproportionately short, and almost skinny. A common trait, he said, among the Cherokee men in his family. I often wondered how his legs could support his heavily muscled upper body.

"Well?" I said.

"Got anything to smoke?"

There were two cigarettes in a pack on the table by the bed. I removed one, lit it, and then threw the package at MacDuff.

"She's there alright," MacDuff said. "At the Ballenger house."

"How do you know?"

"I went there, and spoke to Billy. He'd already made friends with the coachman."

"Have Billy and Dixon got everything under control?"

"It's an easy house to watch."

MacDuff lit his cigarette, and tossed the empty package back. He blew smoke at me from across the room.

"According to the morning edition, Miss Anthony will speak at half past seven this evening. The Liberal Club on College Avenue at the corner of Third Street."

"That agrees with the information on our list," I said.

MacDuff got up and prepared to leave. I squashed the cigarette package into a hard little ball. I threw it as he was going out the door, hitting him squarely on the back of the head.

He looked around, and made a face.

"You know, Millicent, those Eugenicists we saw the other day believe Nordic types should prevail. You know, blond hair, blue eyes…"

"What do you mean?" I said.

"Well, Millicent, at least I have one blue eye."

I shouted a mild expletive at him.

After breakfasting at the hotel café, we drove to the Liberal Club. There was no one there at eight o'clock in the morning, not even the janitor.

We did a thorough investigation of the premises outside, and then sat down on a bench near the entrance to wait for a staff person with a key. Soon, a tall young thing arrived and let herself in. We waited a few minutes, and then went to the door.

"Okay, Millicent," MacDuff whispered, before we went in. "We're New York City newspaper reporters here to cover Miss Anthony's speech, right?" We went inside.

The young woman at the desk said, "Welcome to the Liberal Club of Poughkeepsie."

We introduced ourselves. I said I was Mary Ann, she said she was Rachael. "My name is Ryan," said MacDuff.

We showed our fake news reporter identification. I explained that we were there to cover Miss Anthony's speech, and would like to see the hall.

"And, we should also like permission to quote you in our article, Rachael, if you would be so kind."

She came briskly out from behind her desk and led us both up a set of stairs to the second story.

At the top of the stairs, Rachael leaned an ample hip against the double entrance doors. The doors opened on the lecture hall, a large room set up with rows of chairs facing a stage upon which stood a podium. The hall would seat two hundred and seventy-five.

Hearing someone come in downstairs, Rachael excused herself and went down to her desk.

"No problem with windows," MacDuff said. "They're too high off the ground. That door at the center of the wall, behind the lectern..." MacDuff pointed. "It's a little worrisome, but Billy and Dixon can handle it."

Our inspection of the building's exterior had revealed that the door in question led outside to a flight of stairs, and those stairs led down to the back yard. Back downstairs, Rachael showed us the rest of the premises. I thanked her for the guided tour, and MacDuff and I left the Liberal Club.

After about a block, MacDuff stopped in mid-stride. I stopped. He had that look. He was watching another play at Palmer's. After some minutes, MacDuff rejoined me.

"No, Millicent," he said. "Nobody will attempt to assassinate Susan B. Anthony at the Poughkeepsie Liberal Club this evening. There's no way an assassin could kill her, and manage to escape. He'd know one of the four of us would nab him."

We returned to the Liberal Club early, and waited in our carriage. A maroon coach pulled up at the front entrance, paused, then pulled round the corner into the driveway at the left side of the building. It was Miss Anthony. Rachael met her when she stepped down from the coach.

We saw a group of men gathering where the driveway met the street, about a dozen men altogether. They carried signs with anti-suffrage slogans. Two of the men shouted unkind words at Miss Anthony when she got out of the coach. Rachael took Miss Anthony's arm and led her swiftly in through the side door.

"See the bearded man, Millicent?" MacDuff said. "And the one who just shouted the obscenity?"

I nodded.

"Pinkerton men, both of them."

"Paid to harass Miss Anthony?" I said, incredulously. He nodded.

"How disgusting!"

A policeman idly swinging his baton approached one of the

anti-suffrage men. The policeman said something and the group dispersed. None of them looked like anyone on our suspect list. But I thought one of the men looked like one of the anti-suffrage marchers we had seen near the Cooper Union, one of those men who carried a sign promoting radical Eugenics.

A moment later Billy Bergin's face appeared at the side window of our coach. MacDuff opened the door, and Billy stepped in.

"Where's Dixon?" MacDuff said.

"Out back watching the stairs."

MacDuff nodded approvingly.

"Any last minute orders, MacDuff?"

"You and Dixon saw those men the coppers told to leave?"

"Yes we saw them, MacDuff."

"Recognize any of them?"

"No."

Billy stayed near the front entrance to watch the people come in. MacDuff and I pinned our newspaper identification badges to our lapels, and went inside and up the stairs to the lecture hall. MacDuff took the aisle seat to the right of the double entrance doors, in the back row. I took the aisle seat in the front row directly across from the speaker's platform.

The hall quickly filled, with women mostly, and a few gentlemen from high up the Poughkeepsie social register. Diamond rings and stick pins glittered throughout the hall. Just before the hall door closed, a group of working women came in and took back row seats. There was not a lot of glitter among their little assembly.

No one in the audience looked like a murderer. No one looked like the men Monk had named, and whom Billy had described. Nor did anyone remind MacDuff of the face he saw looking in the window in Brooklyn.

Miss Anthony finished her speech to loud applause.

A woman in a large hat delayed us at the bottom of the stairs on our way out. She held in her hand like a bouquet a collection of colorful pamphlets. The woman thrust a pamphlet in my face, then when I raised my arm in a reflex action, she expertly guided the pamphlet into my palm. My hand closed round it automatically. The woman shoved a pamphlet into the hand of the next person. I passed down the stairs to the lobby, looking for MacDuff who had gone down ahead.

In the lobby I stood aside to look more closely at the pamphlet. It was tastefully designed, overall. The front panel depicted an elegantly dressed young couple, their faces tilted romantically toward each other. I unfolded the pamphlet. The information on the two inside panels was, shall I say-interesting? It was about birth control. What is more, there were drawings illustrating what the printed matter had already made quite clear. One needn't use one's imagination. In large, bold face type, it proclaimed, "Now you know, now you can choose!" Next to the words was a drawing of a woman smiling.

Under the ridiculous Comstock Obscenity laws, it was illegal to print or distribute birth control information, so I was duly impressed with the young woman who dared hand me the pamphlet. Had there been a policeman present, he would have arrested the brave pamphleteer on the spot as he would a common criminal, and carted her off to jail. I put the pamphlet in my shoulder bag.

I intended to ask the woman for an interview using my fake newspaper credentials. But before I could catch up with her a coach pulled up at the curb, and carried away the brave pamphleteer. Watching the coach leave, I thought I saw two faces looking out the rear window. One face was that of the courageous lady, the other was a man.

I met MacDuff outside. "Someone gave me this." I showed him the pamphlet.

"The woman on the stairs?"

"Yes."

Reaching inside his coat, MacDuff showed me an identical pamphlet.

"She took a hell of a chance, Millicent."

"Yes, the Comstock Laws. She looked familiar, MacDuff."

"That woman we saw with the protesters, the mother of

birth control -- remember Millicent?"

"Of course! Mabel Singer. I couldn't tell, because her hat covered most of her face."

MacDuff and I turned just in time to see the coach with Miss Anthony in it come out of the driveway, then turn onto College Street and drive away. Moments later Billy and Dixon's coach appeared, and followed Miss Anthony's coach down the street.

Miss Anthony would speak next in Albany, day after tomorrow at seven-thirty in the evening.

In the morning there was a special delivery letter waiting for us at the front desk. MacDuff tucked the letter in his pocket. We went out and hired the first cab in the hack line. As soon as we were underway, MacDuff handed the letter to me.

"Oh, oh," I said.

"Uh huh. Just open it, Millicent. Please," MacDuff said, clenching his teeth.

I slipped my nail under the flap and broke the black sealing wax. My heart skipped a beat. I turned the letter over and studied the typewritten address. It looked like the typing on the envelope Belle gave us in New York City. The message was brief. I read it silently.

"Oh, Blast." I said, handing the letter to MacDuff. He read it aloud.

> *"Mr. MacDuff,*
> *Sorry I missed you at Justus Schwab's. Perhaps I'll run into you after all, sometime soon. Or maybe I'll run into your lovely assistant instead, in Albany -- now there's a Capital idea! As for protecting Miss Anthony, well you might as well give up on that notion."*

"Mailed from Albany, according to the postmark," I said, "at three o'clock this morning. Unsigned. No return street address."

I dug down into the bottom of my bag and retrieved the

letter Belle had given us. Obviously, the same typewriting machine had been used to compose both letters.

"He must haul that machine around with him!" MacDuff said.

MacDuff held the letter up to the side window. I looked over his shoulder. The paper was of the same high quality, and some of the typewriter keys had perforated the page.

"MacDuff," I said, "I believe these letters prove that the person we're after is insane!"

MacDuff looked at me. "Millicent," he said. "There's a man in Vienna, an alienist, named Dr. Freud. He wrote an article about crazy people who write letters and don't sign them. Our man isn't like those crazy people. This Dr. Freud says they're mostly uneducated middle-aged women, and the letters they write focus mostly on sex matters."

"MacDuff," I said, embarrassed, "have you ever stopped to consider that you read too much?"

The cab pulled up at the depot entrance. Stepping down from the carriage with my grip I went inside and purchased my ticket, then sat down on a bench. MacDuff, as planned, came in soon after. He purchased his ticket and sat down at the other end of the depot with a newspaper. Holding it up in front of his face, he pretended to read.

Today MacDuff, completely out of character, was a traveling businessman wearing a striped shirt and stiff white collar. He had even polished his shoes -- well, the tips of the toes. I was a school marm from Atlanta. I had on a boxy short-waist jacket. Pince-nez glasses perched on my nose. I had affected a quaint Atlanta school marm's southern drawl.

Looking over at MacDuff, I smiled. It occurred to me that the only time MacDuff dressed like other men was when he was on a case in disguise.

Chapter 15

The train that would take us to Albany rumbled into the station. Finally, along came Miss Anthony. Followed by a porter, Miss Anthony marched to a passenger car where the conductor helped her aboard. I saw Billy and Dixon climb onto the car behind hers. MacDuff boarded Miss Anthony's car.

We pulled into the Albany station at lunchtime. A woman in a coach met Miss Anthony soon as she detrained. Billy and Dixon followed them from the station. MacDuff and I followed Billy and Dixon.

Miss Anthony's route went out of the city, then up a long hill into farming country. Her coach turned off the main road, then went down a lane leading to a farmhouse. Miss Anthony and the other woman entered the house, followed by the coachman with Miss Anthony's luggage.

A thick grove of trees stood near the lane that led to the house. Perfect cover for Billy and Dixon who must watch the house through the long night. But Billy and Dixon drove some distance past the lane, then stopped by the side of the road behind more trees. MacDuff stopped our coach behind theirs. We got out of our coach and climbed in with Billy and Dixon.

"You saw where she went," Billy said.

"We did," I said.

Miss Anthony would speak Saturday evening at the Grange Hall, located about a mile back where the street changed from cobblestones to dirt. Near the Grange was the Capital House Hotel. A tavern, really, with rooms to let upstairs. We told our agents that we would stay the night there.

After a brief conference, we left Billy and Dixon to watch the farmhouse, and we drove back to the Grange Hall, where a close inspection of the place revealed no serious security problems.

On our way to secure our rooms, we were distracted by a noisy commotion coming from a side street. MacDuff, always curious, pulled back on the reins. Turning onto the side street, we saw a group of women marching up and down in front of a manufacturer of lady's corsets. One of the marchers looked familiar.

"MacDuff," I said, "that woman?"

"Yeah, Emma Goldberg," MacDuff said.

When the marchers broke up, I got out of the carriage and called to Miss Goldberg, who then had her back to us.

"Emma! Emma Goldberg. Over here!"

Squinting against the sun, she looked in our direction.

"Millicent! Miss Millicent, my sister!" she said, rushing toward me.

Soon all three of us were dining together at the Capital House.

"You are here in Albany for to keep Miss Anthony safe?"

"We are," I said.

"And you're here to make trouble for the capitalist gangster who owns the corset factory?" MacDuff grinned. Emma Goldberg laughed heartily.

The large man I saw standing behind the bar when we came in strode over to our table.

Miss Goldberg introduced us. "Miss Millicent and Mr. MacDuff, my good friends from Lower East Side," she said.

"This big man, who never does he smile, is comrade Franz. Is half capitalist by blood, and owns this Capital House."

MacDuff finished his dinner quickly, then excused himself, claiming he was tired and would now go to his room to relax.

Emma and I smoked cigarettes and talked. Unfortunately nothing useful to our case came of my talk with Emma. Afterwards, Emma went to the home of a friend where she would stay the night. I went to MacDuff's second-floor room, which was next to mine. I raised my arm and made a fist to knock.

"Come in, Millicent." MacDuff's muffled voice came through the door. I jumped.

I opened the door, and found MacDuff sitting in an armchair. An oil lamp burned on the table next to the chair, the flame so bright I had to shade my eyes with my hand.

"How did you know this time that I was at the door, MacDuff?" I closed the door behind me.

"Who else but my fair Millicent?"

"What if it had been the assassin instead, MacDuff, and you with the door unlocked? I am surprised at your negligence!"

When my eyes adjusted to the bright light, I saw a book open face down on MacDuff's lap. With his left hand, MacDuff turned down the lamp, and then set the book on the table. Something in his right hand caught the lamplight. A revolver, pointed straight at me!

"So if you'd been the assassin…" MacDuff's voice trailed off.

"Damn you, MacDuff."

I sat down in the chair facing his. MacDuff put the revolver away. Lighting a cigarette, I leaned over and blew smoke in MacDuff's face. He waved the smoke away.

"Well, what did you find out, Millicent?"

"Exactly nothing."

"Did she mention Berkholdt?"

"Emma says he's en route to Pittsburgh. She says Sasha is upset with how Andrew Carnegie's right hand man treats workers."

"Man by the name of Fricke?"

"Yes. Emma says Berkholdt went to Pittsburgh to make trouble for him."

"Fricke deserves trouble. Has Emma heard anything about the assassination plot since leaving Manhattan, even rumors?"

"No, MacDuff. Sorry."

People began filing into the hall at seven o'clock, and there were no angry men on the street. The Albany audience was different. There were farmers' wives, some with babes in arms. There were older children, too, with straw clinging to their britches. There were women from the nearby factories, strong women, proud women, immigrant women plainly dressed.

The Grange Hall filled up. A woman of grand proportions, bustled and corseted, gray-haired and stern-faced, strode down the aisle from the entrance doors, climbed up three steps, marched across the platform, and planted herself solidly behind the lectern.

She stood and stared stiffly at the audience. "Old Ironsides," I thought to myself, and smiled. She had that look about her.

Reaching under the lectern, she brought out a gavel. She raised the gavel, paused it midair, and smashed it down with enough force, I thought, to splinter the lectern. Now the crowd was silent, and I sat down.

Moments later, I caught a glimpse of black fabric, and heard the swish of skirts. It might have been Queen Victoria, herself, in all her finery, rather than this plain looking old Quaker woman with the deep-set eyes walking down the center aisle. The crowd was utterly still. You could have heard the proverbial pin.

At the end of the speech, before the applause died to mere thunder, Ironsides took Miss Anthony by the hand and whisked her out the Grange Hall side door.

Hurrying outside ahead of the crowd, I saw a coach come down the driveway toward me, and as it passed I caught sight of Miss Anthony and another woman inside. MacDuff appeared at my side.

"Where did she go?" he said.

"There," I pointed.

Miss Anthony's coach turned onto the street, and drove rapidly toward the farmhouse where she would sleep again tonight. A carriage darted out from the curb behind the coach, Billy and Dixon, following Miss Anthony home.

Many people milled about in front of the Grange Hall; among them was a familiar face: Mrs. Singer. She was handing out her pamphlets. Then I saw another familiar face: Miss Emma Goldberg. Emma walked over, said something to Mabel Singer, who handed a package to Emma, who smiled and went away.

Something occurred to me then that had not crossed my mind before. I joined MacDuff, who was standing nearby. Keeping my voice low, I said:

"MacDuff, what if the assassin were a…"

"A woman, Millicent, instead of a man? I've wondered too."

"Do you think it likely?"

"I won't go that far."

"But it could be a woman," I said excitedly. History and literature have shown us plenty of examples."

"Yeah, Millicent, your kind definitely has what it takes to do the deed. Lucretia Borgia comes to mind."

"Or Lizzie Borden, the axe murderer," I said.

Something I once read about Mabel Singer came to mind.

"MacDuff, did you know that before the war Mabel Singer's father was one of the biggest landowners in the South, and owned hundreds of slaves?"

"But, who would hire her, Millicent? Certainly not those radical Eugenicists. They'd think, because she's a woman, that she'd be too dumb for the job."

I disagreed. I thought the Eugenicists would use any means available to achieve their goals.

Chapter 16

Back at the Capital House we had dinner in my room, and after the waiter cleared, we reviewed the case.

We asked, once again, the age-old questions: Who, What, When, Where and Why, and How; then we explored possible answers.

"Well, Millicent," MacDuff said. "Miss Anthony has given speeches in Brooklyn, Poughkeepsie, and now Albany, and so far nobody's succeeded in killing her."

"But we know somebody wants to."

"We know there's a plot, yes. We know the what, but that's all we know. So who wants to kill her?"

I shook my head.

"We don't know who, we don't know when, we don't know where, and we sure don't know how or why," MacDuff said.

"Well, we do have suspects, MacDuff."

"You mean Joey Sharpe, and those other hoodlum names Johnny Monk gave us? We already agreed those guys aren't real suspects. They're names, that's all. And we know those two anarchist lovebirds, Goldberg and Berkholdt, probably don't have anything to do with the plot either."

"Well, MacDuff, are you sure?"

"When they saw us at Justus Schwab's they ran out the back door, yes, but that doesn't necessarily make them suspects"

"But that same night, right after we left Justus Schwab's, somebody driving a closed unlighted coach with rubber-shod horses and rubber-tired wheels tried to kill you. It could have been Emma or Berkholdt, or both of them."

"That coach and pair cost something, Millicent, more than two penniless anarchists could afford."

"Maybe, MacDuff, just maybe they are in the pay of a wealthy co-conspirator."

"And their motive, Millicent?"

"To get us out of the way, to more easily get at Miss

Anthony."

"But there we are again, Millicent." MacDuff threw both hands up. "No motive! Why would two anarchists want to kill Susan B. Anthony, a famous activist known to agree with some of the Anarchist platform, and has even given it public support?"

"Well, MacDuff, we know there has to be a motive. Even if a madman kills somebody, he benefits from it in some way. If only for the thrill of it. Even you said that the person who writes the letters wants to kill Miss Anthony, at least in part, for the bloody thrill of it.

"MacDuff, what if it's Berkholdt, and he is a madman? I mean someone who would be diagnosed as such by one of those alienists, such as your Dr. Freud. Actually, MacDuff, Berkholdt is rather new to our area. Remember when Emma told us his story, that he'd come to America only a few months ago from Vilna?"

"Anyhow, Millicent, I don't think Berkholdt's a madman. Neither is Emma Goldberg. They're fanatics. That's what Professor James would call them, no doubt about that. But they're not crazy. Of course, there's the self-styled mother of birth control," MacDuff said.

"Oh, MacDuff, don't be so crude!" I was tired of his jokes about Mrs. Singer. "That brave person is doing something good for all women!"

"Millicent, I'm interested in the man whose face we saw at the back window of Mabel Singer's coach when she left the lecture hall in Poughkeepsie. I'd spend a lot of Belle's money to find out who it was."

"But, MacDuff, all we saw was a face with no distinguishing features."

MacDuff scratched his chin.

"You know, Millicent, since this little play began our birth control pamphleteer has been in almost every scene."

"Except the one that played back in Brooklyn," I said. "Emma Goldberg wasn't there either. But we knew she wouldn't be, because she told us."

MacDuff scratched his chin. "So do these two characters,

both of them women, both of them dedicated to her cause, have a common cause which we don't know anything about? But which just might involve a plot to kill Susan B. Anthony?"

After further discussion, we decided that Emma Goldberg was not a likely suspect. But we still could not entirely rule out Mabel Singer.

"Maybe it's the pamphleteer acting alone," MacDuff said.

Ultimately, we ruled out Mabel Singer too, because we couldn't think of a likely motive.

"Millicent, maybe there's another reason that both those radical females keep showing up where Miss Anthony does a speech."

We decided that it did, indeed, make sense. Miss Anthony has been involved with many radical groups since the first women's rights meeting in Seneca Falls, NY. That was 1848, a long time ago. She was an abolitionist, and later joined the anti-Saloon League. One of her closest friends, Elizabeth Cady Stanton, is a socialist. Mrs. Cady Stanton and Miss Anthony once published a newspaper called The Revolution. Miss Anthony has even shared the speaker's platform with the likes of Victoria Woodhull, a radical socialist who, strangely enough, was rumored to have once advocated forced sterilization of so-called defectives.

"Miss Anthony has even been on friendly terms with some of the milder anarchists," MacDuff said, "and she also supports the labor union movement. Millicent, Emma Goldberg is an outspoken anarchist, yet Miss Anthony counts Goldberg as a friend to the cause of Suffrage. Mabel Singer's a birth control advocate. Two radical women, each with her own strong message. Best way to spread their message to a lot of people..."

"Of course!" I said. "Ride on Miss Anthony's skirts! She draws crowds wherever she goes. In mill towns like Poughkeepsie and Albany, she draws young women who work in the mills. Those are exactly the people Emma Goldberg and Mabel Singer are trying to reach. Emma with her anarchist labor union cause, Mabel Singer with her birth control pamphlets."

It had grown dark while we talked. We turned up the gas and lit the lamps next to our chairs.

"Well, MacDuff, regarding the case as it stands, may I offer my summary?"

"Tell me, Millicent."

"First, I want to say that I believe our cast of characters is, as yet, incomplete. I do not think the person who wrote those two letters is anyone we have seen so far."

"But you think the person who wrote the letters, and the would-be assassin, are one and the same?" MacDuff said.

"Yes," I said.

"I think you might be right, Millicent. Maybe whoever it is hasn't stepped on stage yet." MacDuff leaned back in his chair. "Or maybe we just haven't noticed."

"Listen, MacDuff," I said. "Let's say somebody in the Suffrage movement is jealous of Miss Anthony's power." I paused a minute, to think. "This person wants Miss Anthony out of the way so she can take over the movement and usurp Miss Anthony's power. Most Suffragettes, not just the leaders of the Suffrage movement, but the masses of them, are against the Liquor Industry."

MacDuff gave an exaggerated flinch. I made a fist and reached over and punched him on the shoulder.

"Powerful individuals in the liquor business are afraid that, if Suffrage succeeds, women would eventually vote en masse to prohibit the sale of alcoholic beverages in this country. I knew you wouldn't like that connection, MacDuff, but it is a feasible one.

"And here is another possible motive for killing the great lady. MacDuff, American women, far more than men, support liberal causes. A powerful group of conservative politicians has taken stock of the situation. They know that with Miss Anthony's leadership women will in time win the right to vote. These same conservative men would likely lose their power. Therefore, they have hatched a plot to kill Miss Anthony and destroy the Suffrage movement in order to hold onto their power!"

"But who is the hired gun, Millicent?"

MacDuff leaned toward me. "Is it Monk?"

"As I see it, we don't even need to know his name,"

MacDuff."

"You're right, partner," MacDuff said. "And we don't have to know his motive either."

MacDuff' brown eye was closed. He was staring at me with that cold blue eye.

"Yeah," he said. "We don't have to know his name or why he wants to kill Miss Anthony."

"But we have to stop him, and that's all we have to know."

"Yes, MacDuff, that's our primary task. We were hired to stop the assassin, whoever he may be, from killing Miss Anthony. Everything else is superfluous."

"Yeah, Millicent," MacDuff said. "We have to keep her alive, no matter what!"

After MacDuff left, I sat and reread some of Nellie Bly's interview with Miss Anthony. Then I turned down the gas, blew out the lamps and crawled into bed.

But before we had left Manhattan, MacDuff had said: "No booze for MacDuff 'till this case is solved." Then he looked at me out of that cold blue eye, and said, "And no laudanum dreams for Millicent."

It was a "fair deal," according to MacDuff. I acquiesced.

In the morning at breakfast, MacDuff had just finished a plate of bacon and eggs when he slammed his fist down on the table. Franz, who seemed to embody the entire Capital House staff that morning, looked up from where he stood behind the bar reading the morning paper.

"Damn, give me a straight-from-the-shoulder murder case any day, even a jewel robbery!"

"You needn't be so histrionic, MacDuff," I said, embarrassed by his outburst.

"Something wrong with your eggs, Mister?" Franz said from behind the bar.

"Don't mind him, Franz," I said. "Actually, when MacDuff pounds the table like that, it means the eggs were done just as he likes."

Franz came to our table with fresh coffee.

"Yeah, thanks, Franz," MacDuff said, "and Millicent's right, the eggs were perfect."

Chapter 17

Just then, Billy Bergin came through the dining room doors. He hurried to our table and sat down, looking haggard and drawn.

"Miss Millicent, MacDuff."

"You don't look so good, Billy," MacDuff said. "What's wrong?"

"You wouldn't look so good either, after a night like Dixon and I had," Billy said.

Franz came and set a clean cup and a carafe of fresh coffee on the table. Billy filled his cup, spooned in some sugar.

"Okay, Billy," MacDuff said. "Let's hear it."

"About four o'clock this morning a man driving a carriage with the top thrown back came racing down the road towards the clump of trees where Dixon and I were hiding. It was Dixon's turn to sleep, so I woke him up."

"When he went past, the driver threw this from out of the carriage."

Billy handed MacDuff an object wrapped in butcher paper and tied with brown cord. MacDuff loosened the cord and removed the paper, revealing what looked like a knife grip.

"Careful, MacDuff," Billy said.
Billy swigged some coffee. He wiped his mouth with his hand. His right eye twitched.

Pointing the object at the ceiling, MacDuff pressed a button. An eight-inch blade shot straight out. MacDuff pressed the button again. The blade slid back inside the handle, like a snake retreating into its hiding place ready to strike again.

"My, how nice," I said. "May I see it?"

MacDuff handed me the weapon, and I examined it. The knife looked deadly, and it could be easily concealed in a man's pocket or a woman's handbag. I set it down on the table.

MacDuff handed me the sheet of paper in which the stiletto had been wrapped.

"What did the man driving the carriage look like?" MacDuff

leaned close to Billy.

"The moon was behind him and he was wearing one of those big hats, MacDuff, so it was hard to tell. He looked like one of those silhouette cutouts."

"Was he tall or short, slim or heavy?"

"I couldn't tell about his build. He had on a real long bulky coat."

"What about him did you notice, Billy, that could help you or Dixon identify him if you ever saw him again?"

"I can't be sure, MacDuff, neither could Dixon."

"Did you try to follow him?"

"No, we stayed put. I figured that maybe he wanted us to follow him. But if we had, then with Dixon and me out of the way, an accomplice, if he had one, could've broken into the house and killed Miss Anthony."

"Good thinking, Billy."

MacDuff handed me the sheet of paper that had been attached to the knife.

"Why me, MacDuff?"

"Read, Millicent," He said. "Please."

"It's the same, MacDuff," I said.

"I know!"

Like the others, the letter was typewritten on the same expensive paper, but in this case there was no envelope. I turned the letter over.

"Blast!" I said.

The black seal was partially broken. I finished breaking it using my fingernail, then I unfolded the letter. Holding it to the light, I glanced at the typewritten characters.

"Same machine, same heavy hand," I said.

MacDuff said something in Cherokee under his breath.

"The same obscene sort of message, too."

I read the letter aloud, softly, so other patrons would not overhear.

"Good morning, MacDuff,
Still think you can stop me? How stupid! You don't even know what I look like. I'll see you and your nigger helper in Syracuse. I'll be the unlikely person at the edge of the crowd."

"Unsigned, no date, damn these letters!" I said.

Snatching the letter from me, MacDuff closed his hand around it, and squeezed down hard. The muscles bulged under his shirt. Soon the message would be unreadable pulp.

"MacDuff, no!" I said.

He stopped, took a deep breath, exhaled. "Evidence, Millicent, yeah, I know."

He gave the mangled message back to me. I smoothed out the paper and carefully refolded it. I placed the letter down in the bottom of my bag with the others we had collected.

"As you know, Billy, this isn't the first letter we've gotten from him," MacDuff said.

Billy's right eyelid twitched crazily. He looked at his watch.

"She'll be heading for the station soon," he said. "I better go." Billy left to rejoin Dixon at the farmhouse.

"Okay, Millicent," MacDuff's mood had improved. "Syracuse is next. Then Seneca Falls, then?"

"Rochester, MacDuff. Followed by Buffalo, and finally…"

"Spooksville." MacDuff looked at me.

"That's not nice, MacDuff," I chided.

He grew quiet.

"Why so pensive all of a sudden?" I said, touching MacDuff's arm.

"Millicent, I'm scared. For our descendants. This case isn't just about keeping Susan B. Anthony alive so American women can vote someday."

Chapter 18

No suspicious characters boarded the train in Albany, and none got on at any of the whistle stops on the way to Syracuse. Billy and Dixon followed Miss Anthony from the Syracuse station, to the home of the President of the Women's College where Miss Anthony would speak.

MacDuff and I found rooms to let at an establishment near the college called the Adirondack Inn. It seemed a friendly place. In the common room was an enormous fireplace, "Big enough," MacDuff remarked, "to host a crap game." The furniture was heavy and rustic, which I thought fit in well with the rest of the decor. When I asked MacDuff's opinion, which I understood at once to have been a mistake, he said, "Looks like a gang of beavers got let loose on that furniture." The manager, who had overheard, made an unpleasant face. He said the furniture was Adirondack style.

Climbing into bed that night I reread another chapter from Nellie Bly's Susan B. Anthony article, wishing all the while that I had a full time writing job with the *New York Sun*, and an editor who would send me on exciting assignments.

Suddenly it dawned on me. I set the article aside.

"Millicent Davies!" I said aloud to the walls of my room. "You are on an assignment at this very moment which would turn Nellie Bly green with envy. To stop an assassin from killing the most celebrated woman in recent history, now what assignment could possibly be more exciting than that!"

I turned down my lamp, and within minutes fell asleep. When I woke, I found I had slept the night through without mussing the bedclothes.

MacDuff and I breakfasted in the Adirondack dining room. MacDuff surveyed the dining room furnishings.

"I see the same gang of beavers got loose in here, too" he remarked.

At the college lecture hall that night, students and staff received Miss Anthony's message with enthusiasm. Everything else about the Syracuse event, I thought at the time, was unremarkable. And there were no angry men outside the hall shouting obscenities at Miss Anthony.

Back at the Inn, we talked about Miss Anthony's speech, agreeing that it was one of her best. We also agreed it made perfect sense that neither Mrs. Singer nor Miss Goldberg was there. The audience was all wrong. Emma Goldberg appeals to women who work in the factories and mills. No such women go to the Women's College. The mother of birth control gives her free pamphlets to poor women from the cities. Students at that high-priced college, we concluded, could buy birth control information from their family doctor.

Later, Billy showed up at the Inn with his report, which was by no means routine. It centered, for the most part, on a single event. Billy spotted somebody leaving the lecture hall who, for two reasons, stood out from the crowd.

"First of all," Billy said, "it was a man. Secondly, he didn't have a woman on his arm."

"Go on, Billy." MacDuff lit a cigarette.

"Well, I couldn't help but think of that letter. Remember the part where it says something like, 'I'll be the unlikely guy at the edge of the crowd?'"

"Yeah, Billy, I remember."

"Anyhow, I was standing just outside the main door. Dixon was watching the side door. A lot of other people stood around waiting for Miss Anthony to come out. The man I saw, who looked maybe thirty years old, was standing on the sidewalk near the driveway. There was a streetlamp where the sidewalk met the driveway.

"He did look kind of out of place standing there alone, MacDuff. At first, I thought he might've been a newspaperman. But, no, I said to myself, he was dressed more like some Joe just out for a stroll. Then he lit a cigarette. That gave me an opportunity, him lighting up. I stuck a cigarette in my mouth, and, MacDuff, I got a quick look at him when I went and asked for a light."

"Yeah Billy, c'mon give!"

"The guy was, as I said, about thirty. I'd put him at five foot five, and about one-thirty-five. Trim, not paunchy. As I said, dressed like a Joe out for a stroll. An ordinary Joe, MacDuff. Maybe a factory rat by day. His suit looked cheap, and he had on a dingy white shirt, and no collar.

"But, MacDuff, I think his front was phony. I mean, the suit pants were baggy at the knees, as you'd expect from a cheap suit. But they were too baggy. Another thing was, his hat didn't match the cheap suit. It was nicely blocked, and way too expensive. Like the letter said, he was the unlikely one.

"Now here's the important part, MacDuff. I got a good look at his hands when he set fire to my cigarette. His hands looked like mine, only better than mine. Remember what I said about Jack Raven's hands? Looked like he'd just been to one of those uptown tonsorial joints where they take about an hour to trim and polish your nails.

"Anyway, MacDuff, I thought he looked like a guy with more than a few Morgan's in his pocket who was trying to look hard-up. More like the factory boss than a hired hand. So I asked myself, what's a man like that doing hanging around this all-girl's college, where Miss Anthony did this speech tonight on Women's Suffrage?"

"Where is this man now?" I said.

"Wish I knew, Millicent. Soon as he lit my cigarette, he wished me good evening and walked away. I couldn't follow him, because just then Dixon came running up saying Miss Anthony had just got in her coach. A minute later, it came rattling down the driveway. We had to go jump in our carriage and follow her."

"Do you think it was Jack Raven, Billy?" MacDuff said.

"It might've been Raven. His hands sure did look like Raven's hands."

"Think you'd recognize this man if you saw him again, Billy?"

Billy's hand stole to his face. He touched the scar under his eye.

"Yeah, I think so."

In the morning Miss Anthony would board the westbound train, her destination: the village of Seneca Falls.

According to the schedule Mrs. Beecher Hooker had given us, Miss Anthony would change her usual scheduling pattern for the Seneca Falls and Rochester speeches. Instead of waiting till the following day, Miss Anthony would speak in Seneca Falls that evening. Next morning she would travel to the city of Rochester, and would do her speech there in the evening of the same day.

MacDuff pounded on my door just as I was putting on my jacket.

"Millicent!" He yelled through the door.

"What is your big hurry, MacDuff!"

I opened the door. MacDuff shoved an envelope in my hand.

"Oh, no," I said.

"It was partway under your door, Millicent." MacDuff closed the door. I broke the black seal, and removed the one-page insert.

> *"Still think you can stop me, MacDuff? How stupid! I'll see you, and your nigger helper, in Seneca Falls. Oh, there'll be a hot time in the old town…"*

"Why these awful letters, MacDuff?"

"Decoys, Millicent."

"To throw us off?"

"Maybe to make us think we're chasing a madman across New York State. Oh, the race hate is real, alright. But the person we're after is no stupid K.K.K. member."

"No, the way the letters are written proves that."

MacDuff caught my arm. "And look what else I found partway under your door, Millicent."

He pulled a man's dress glove out of his inside pocket.

I took the glove and examined it. It was light grey in color, with hand stitching along the back of the glove. A pair of them would be quite expensive. It was a man's glove, but meant for someone with small hands. Could it have belonged to Jack Raven, I wondered. I tried it on. It was only a little too large.

Chapter 19

Billy and Dixon followed Miss Anthony from the Seneca Falls depot to the home of the Quaker family with whom she would stay the night. MacDuff and I drove our rented carriage to the Seneca Falls Hotel, where Miss Anthony would deliver her speech that evening in the hotel dining room. After a thorough investigation of the hotel, inside and out, MacDuff and I felt that the four of us could keep Miss Anthony safe for the brief time she would be there.

The dining room was at street level, and there were only three doors leading outside. MacDuff instructed Billy to watch the main entrance, also the emergency door that led from the dining room to the street. Dixon would watch the rear exit, which led from the kitchen to the street behind the hotel. As surveillance jobs go, I said to MacDuff, it should be an easy one. Maybe too easy, MacDuff had said.

MacDuff and I, inside, would watch the people in the dining room, including the dining room staff. Special permits were obtained, so that additional chairs could be placed at the tables, and folding chairs set up along the walls to seat twice the number of people the dining room was meant to hold. Extraordinary measures for an extraordinary event.

There were more than one hundred fifty Suffrage devotees present. Every chair was occupied. The podium stood roughly ten feet from the swing doors opening on the kitchen. I sat on a folding chair facing the lectern about ten feet away. MacDuff sat near the dining room front entrance, with his back against the wall, and could watch everyone in the place.

Miss Anthony had been at the podium perhaps a quarter of an hour, when the kitchen doors burst open. The cook ran out yelling "Fire! Fire!" Thick black smoke rolled out of the kitchen. The kitchen doors swung shut. The smoke spread quickly through the dining room.

Pandemonium ensued. I jumped up. People ran screaming to and fro, knocking over tables and chairs. The woman who had introduced Miss Anthony rushed her out of the dining room through a side door. I knew Billy was outside watching that door. The kitchen doors swung open again. Yet more smoke rolled out. A tall man with handlebar mustaches, dressed all in white, looking like one of the hotel kitchen staff, stepped out from behind the smoke. The doors swung shut behind him.

Reaching under his white cook's jacket, he pulled out a gun. Waving the gun side to side, slowly, he studied the panic-stricken crowd, searching for but one person, Miss Susan B. Anthony!

I snatched my gun from under my coat. In my side vision, I saw MacDuff fighting against the crowd, trying to reach the gunman. The gunman saw MacDuff. I aimed my Iver Johnson at the gunman's chest. Cupping his free hand over his mouth and nose, the gunman spun around and darted back into the kitchen. MacDuff broke through the crowd, sending a man who was in his way sprawling. Rushing past me, MacDuff kicked open the kitchen doors. Orange flames shot out. MacDuff dropped to the floor and rolled away from the flames. The doors swung shut. MacDuff jumped back on his feet. I ran to his side.

"C'mon, Millicent!" he grabbed my arm and pulled me along.

By now, everybody else had escaped from the dining room. MacDuff and I ran through the thick smoke, coughing, through the lobby then out the front door. Two policemen hustled us across the sidewalk to the other side of the street.

The horse-drawn fire engines had already arrived. I had heard them roaring towards the hotel even before we ran outside, heard the pounding of horses hooves on the street.

Billy Bergin came rushing up.

"I can't find Dixon!" Billy shouted.

"There he is!" I pointed.

Dixon came wobbling toward us from across the street, holding his head. I ran to meet him.

"Dixon!" I said. "What's wrong? Let me see."

I put a hand on his shoulder, and looked at a big lump on the back of Dixon's skull. I touched it lightly with my finger.

"Ouch! Damn!" Dixon said.

Billy ran out in the street and joined me, and together we helped Dixon onto the sidewalk where MacDuff stood waiting.

"I got sapped," Dixon said. "Out behind the hotel." He touched the back of his head, and winced.

"Miss Anthony! Where's Miss Anthony!" Losing his balance, Dixon lurched forward like a drunken man. Billy caught his arm, and steadied him.

"Miss Anthony's okay, Dixon," Billy said. "A woman loaded her in a coach. I saw them driving like hell away from the hotel just after the fire broke out."

"Billy," MacDuff said. "You go and watch the Quaker lady's house, where Miss Anthony's staying. Millicent and I will see to Dixon."

Billy placed a hand on Dixon's shoulder.

"You're a good man, my friend," he said. Then he jumped in the carriage hitched to a post nearby, and drove away.

Dixon refused to see a doctor.

"I'm okay," he insisted. "Besides, a doctor would ask all kinda questions, right?"

The Seneca Falls firefighters had already put out the fire. According to one of the policemen, fire damage was confined to the kitchen. It had been gutted by the flames. Luckily, no one was injured, other than Dixon.

"I'm feeling lots more better already," Dixon said. "I been sapped harder'n that by Inspector Byrnes. But I sure could use a cuppa coffee." Dixon pointed at a café sign down the street.

Inside the café, we ordered coffee from the redheaded server. We were the only customers. Everyone else in Seneca Falls was out watching the firemen roll up the hoses.

"Okay, Dixon," MacDuff said after the waitress brought our coffee, "what happened?"

"I was standin' out back of the hotel by the kitchen door. There was factory workers walkin' by on the sidewalk. Whoever sapped me must of been among them people walkin' by, must of snuck up on me when my back was turned."

Dixon touched the back of his head, gently.

I looked at MacDuff. "That's when the gunman went in and set the kitchen on fire."

MacDuff nodded.

"So that's how that fire happened." Dixon hung his sore head.

"Never you mind," MacDuff said. "It wasn't your fault."

"Well, anyways, MacDuff," Dixon went on, "when I woke up the kitchen back door was standin' wide open and there was smoke and flames shootin' out, and I smelt a real strong smell of kerosene.

"I was pretty groggy. But I seen someone run acrossed the street and dive head-first in a coach that was standin' at the curb."

"Was he carrying anything?" MacDuff said.

"He was carryin' a growler, MacDuff! Yeah, it looked like a bucket of beer. But the growler must of been empty. B'cuz when he dove in the carriage, he threw it in 'head of him. You wouldn't do that with a growler what was full."

"That's how he brought the kerosene into the kitchen."

"Right again, Millicent."

Assuring us both that he was now "jist fine," Dixon left the café. He would, he said, "hire a cab and go join Billy."

Talking about the events of the night, after Dixon left, MacDuff and I both wondered why we had not seen Miss Goldberg or Mrs. Singer. The audience had not been 'all wrong,' as was the case in Syracuse. Some of the women in the hotel dining room were employees from the Seneca Falls canning factories.

Back at the hotel where MacDuff and I had booked rooms near the depot, we bade each other goodnight. I crawled in bed and stared at the shadows on the ceiling until I fell asleep, exhausted.
In the morning, Billy joined us for breakfast in my room. We had plenty to talk about. Dixon, Billy reported, was okay this morning.

"He doesn't even have a headache! See why I hired him?"

Billy said.

When we got to the depot, I sent a wire to the Lily Dale Grand Hotel, to reserve rooms so that we would not end up without accommodations when we got there.

"Millicent," MacDuff said, as we boarded the train, "I woke up a coupla' times in the night. Every time I woke, I could see in my mind the final line from the latest letter."

I looked at him.

"…Oh, *there'll be a hot time in the old town…*' remember, Millicent?"

"I'll never forget those words, MacDuff!"

The morning paper carried a front-page story of the fire. The story mentioned that Miss Anthony had been present, and had escaped unharmed, but the reporter said that, regrettably, he had been unable to gain an interview with the famous Suffragette. Police believed that the fire was the work of an arsonist ('Brilliant deduction, Inspector Lestrade!').

Chapter 20

In the morning, I wanted to stop at the Quaker residence to see if we could reason with Miss Anthony, possibly even persuade her to postpone the rest of her tour.

MacDuff closed his brown eye. "You know it wouldn't do any good," he said.

I knew he was right.

The train ride from Seneca Falls to Rochester, which had long been Miss Anthony's permanent residence, took two and one half hours.

The train rolled through the Rochester suburbs, then crawled through downtown to the depot on the city's north side. A sign along the tracks said Welcome to the Flour City, so nicknamed for the many flourmills along the banks of the Genesee River which flows through the city center. We chose a hotel also called the Flour City, just a few blocks from the Masonic Temple Fellowship Hall where Miss Anthony would speak in the evening.

Of course, Miss Anthony would stay with her sister at the family home. As usual, Billy and Dixon followed her from the depot.

Before hiring our carriage, MacDuff sent off a wire from the Western Union Office next to the depot.

"Who was that one for, one of your Pinkerton pals?" I said when he came out.

"Nope, an old professor friend of mine from NYU."

I knew MacDuff had taken some classes at NYU, but I wondered why he would wire one of his old professors. Once more, he read my mind.

"Old Professor Wells, Millicent."

"Wasn't he an expert on political organizations, especially the more radical ones?"

"That's him. He knows more about anarchists and bolshies, and others of their ilk than the State Department."

We found a café, ate a hurried lunch, and then went to

see Miss Anthony's family home. Every person in Rochester knew Miss Anthony's address. Including the café owner, who gave us directions.

"Number Seventeen Madison Street," he said. MacDuff pulled out his Rochester City map, and looked it up.

Using our map, we easily found Madison Street. We drove slowly down Madison, then stopped at the curb on the left side of the street.

"There it is, MacDuff!" I said, excitedly. "The red house, over there on the other side of the street."

It was a modest two-story house of red brick, with cream-colored shutters. Number seventeen was painted on one of the front porch posts. A white picket fence ran waist high along the front. A three-window bay with white curtains jutted out at the top of the house. It was the fabled attic workroom where Miss Anthony did her writing. During the Civil War, the Anthony house was a stop on the Underground Railroad.

"Look," MacDuff said.

Standing at the curb further down Madison, on our side of the street, was a small closed wagon.

MacDuff touched the horse with the whip. We moved down the street and stopped next to the wagon. A sign on the side of the wagon said Knife Sharpening. MacDuff handed me the reins. He got out of the carriage and knocked on the little wooden door at the rear of the wagon. The door opened, and Billy Bergin's smiling face appeared. He stepped out of the wagon, and he and MacDuff climbed into our carriage.

Billy said he had rented it from a man near the train depot.

"There's a little grinder in there." Billy pointed at the wagon. "I've already made good use of it." Billy laughed and pulled a well-honed stiletto out of the sheath on his belt.

"You and Dixon are certainly creative, Billy," I said.

"Thank you, Miss Millicent."

"Where's Dixon, by the way?" MacDuff asked.

"My partner in crime? He's out back of Miss Anthony's house. He got himself a job weeding Miss Anthony's neighbor's garden."

"Things look okay, Billy?" MacDuff asked.

"Things are nice and quiet. How does the hall look?"

"We're heading there now. By the way we're staying at the Flour City, a small hotel not far from the hall."

"The one on Genesee Street? I saw it, MacDuff."

Billy got out of the carriage and back into the wagon. There was a small window in the side of the wagon. Billy smiled out at us as we pulled away.

Leaving the horse and carriage in the care of the hotel doorman, we went up to our rooms to freshen up. Then we drove to the meeting hall. MacDuff knocked. The door opened. An elderly janitor stood in the doorway with a broom in his hand and a smile on his face.

"We're here from the *New York City Magazine*," MacDuff told the old man, "to cover Miss Anthony's hometown speech. We just wanted to see the hall before hand."

The old man cocked his head to the side, bird-like, squinted, then let us in.

"There ain't much to see," he said. "But go 'head and give yer self's the nickel tour."

The janitor went out to sweep the portico, and the front steps. MacDuff and I looked the hall over. The janitor was right; there was not much to see. Essentially, the hall was like all the other halls we had seen. At first, MacDuff thought the windows at the back would pose a problem, but not so. Miss Anthony stood not more than five feet five inches, so the three high windows behind the lectern were too far above Miss Anthony's head to pose a problem. We finished our investigation, and made our exit while the janitor was dusting the chairs.

We arrived back at the hall half an hour early, and heard someone standing near the entrance say that most of the seats were already occupied. Billy was standing near the front entrance, smoking, when we arrived. Billy said:

"She went in by the side door, just a minute ago. Dixon's already out back of the hall." He spoke without moving his lips.

We went inside, and when we showed our newspaper credentials to the woman at the ticket booth she waved us right in.

"The power of the fake press," I said to MacDuff under my breath.

MacDuff had no trouble securing the aisle seat in the back row. However, I was forced to misrepresent myself. I used my fake credentials to obtain a seat on the aisle in the front row across from the speaker's lectern. I simply strode with authority down the center aisle, reporter's note pad in hand, pencil poised above the pad, and said to the woman who occupied the seat I wanted:

"I am sorry, madam, but I shall have to ask you to look for another place to sit."

The poor woman started to protest.

"I am sorry, madam!" I said, pushing my press card at her.

"Oh! Oh, my dear, yes. I am so very sorry," she stuttered.

Gathering up her things, she moved to the back of the hall where there were still some vacant seats.

The hall soon filled with people, wealthy women, mostly, from Rochester's upper crust. But across the aisle from me sat a group of young working women. One of them, a thin girl of perhaps seventeen, raised a hand to adjust her plain black bonnet. When she did, I saw on the back of her swollen hand the dark red patches, which marked her as a garment worker. The girl caught me staring.

"It looks just like a lobster claw, don't it, lady!"

The women with her glared at me. I looked away, embarrassed.

The woman's hand did resemble a lobster claw. The result of sixteen-hour days standing at the loom.

When Miss Anthony entered the hall, all conversation ceased. The great lady walked ahead of the mistress of ceremonies, climbed three steps up onto the platform, and sat down behind the lectern.

Mrs. Beverly Sibley, who occupied the top of Rochester's pyramid of power, introduced Miss Anthony. The women in the audience, along with the few men, patted the palms of their gloved hands together. The atmosphere made me think of a *Times* article I once read describing an afternoon tea at the Rockefeller's Fifth Avenue mansion.

Miss Anthony ended her speech. Gloved hands softly applauded. Instead of applauding, some of the women waved handkerchiefs. I had expected more. Not from Miss Anthony, she always gives her all. I expected some enthusiasm from her audience. After all, the City of Rochester was Miss Anthony's home. I also expected a noisy gathering in the street, a delegation of anti-suffrage proponents, but there was no such gathering. There were, however, several dozen Rochester policemen milling about in front of the hall.

Miss Anthony walked quickly out of the hall after her speech, then down the stairs to the lobby, with Mrs. Sibley following close behind. MacDuff and I waited for a dozen people to leave, then we went out.

Miss Anthony went directly to the shiny green coach that was at the curb. The driver helped her into the coach, climbed back up into the driver's seat, and drove away. That was that.

MacDuff and I watched Miss Anthony's coach move slowly along in the traffic. About half a block down the street, a carriage pulled away from the curb a little ahead of Miss Anthony's coach. The carriage driver had on a tall black hat and plain black gentleman's clothing.

"There goes Billy Bergin," MacDuff said.

A moment later, another carriage drove out from a side street and fell in behind Miss Anthony's coach. It was Dixon, naturally.

MacDuff and I stood and watched the crowd file out the doors of the hall. Big shiny broughams and landaus, and other expensive coaches pulled up one after the other in front of the hall, forming a sort of hack line for the wealthy. Smartly dressed drivers perched on high seats atop the coaches. Liveried assistants sitting next to the drivers clamored down and helped the ladies climb into plush compartments. The assistants remounted, the drivers drove away.

Climbing aboard a horse-drawn car, unassisted, the little group of garment workers were carted unceremoniously away. We did not expect, nor did we see Emma Goldberg or Mrs. Singer with her pamphlets among the wealthy Rochester crowd.

But as MacDuff and I turned to leave, I saw a man who I thought resembled Alexander Berkholdt. MacDuff kept walking; I stopped to look more closely at the man. He was of medium height, and was standing at the far end of the building watching Miss Anthony's coach move along the street. He removed his hat a moment to shade his eyes, revealing dark hair and a high forehead.

Catching up to MacDuff, I grabbed his arm.

"MacDuff, look! Doesn't that gentleman look like..." I didn't bother to finish. When I turned to point him out, the Berkholdt look-alike was gone. MacDuff looked at me.

"Well?" he said.

"Oh, never mind," I said. "I thought I saw someone, is all."

"Who, Millicent?"

"I thought I saw Alexander Berkholdt."

MacDuff scratched his chin. "Next time we see Emma Goldberg, ask her where Berkholdt was when we were here in Rochester."

"If we ever see Miss Goldberg again."

"We will, Millicent, we will."

We went to the hotel bar. While we were having coffee and discussing the events of the day, a newsboy hawking the *Rochester Sentinel* came in yelling:

"Extra! Extra! Elderly woman killed tonight in North Rochester!"

MacDuff bought a paper. The front-page story told about an old woman who had been killed soon after Miss Anthony's speech. We both were stunned by how much the old woman's front-page picture resembled Miss Anthony. According to the account the victim, a Rochester resident, had been an eccentric old woman who enjoyed impersonating Miss Anthony.

The woman had been walking in a North Rochester neighborhood known to be dangerous after dark and according to the police report was attacked by a person, or persons, unknown just a few blocks from her home. A thief, the police surmised, had struck her on the head and stolen her purse. She died at the scene. It was rumored that some Black and Tan clubs operating in the area provided rooms for opium users. Rochester police speculated that an opium addict desperate for money to supply his habit had probably killed the old woman.

"MacDuff," I said after reading the article, "do you suppose the killer may have been our man? He could have made a mistake. After all, the murder took place within a few blocks of Miss Anthony's home. And, MacDuff, the old lady is certainly a ringer for Miss Anthony."

"Poor old woman," he said.

Following the article about the old woman's murder was a story about yet another murder. According to that article, the second murder victim was a man of around thirty years of age. He was a short man, slender, with brown hair. The killer shot the man once through the head. The body lay outside one of the Black and Tan clubs, just a block from where the old woman's body had been found. No identification was found on the man's body. According to the police, there was no evidence linking the two murders.

"Sounds like Jack Raven," MacDuff said, after he had read the second article.

"Do you suppose Raven was the one who killed the old woman?" I said.

"Anything's possible." MacDuff scratched his chin. "Makes me wonder if the one who shot Raven, if it really was Raven's body the cops found, is the same person who killed Eastman."

"I wondered the same thing, MacDuff! Could it mean there is more than one killer loose in Rochester?"

"Could be, Millicent. Could be," MacDuff said.

Chapter 21

In the morning as I was fastening the straps of my grip, MacDuff pounded on my door.

"Hurry up, Millicent!"

He sounded distraught. I opened the door. He strode inside my room. Kicking the door shut with his heel, he thrust an envelope at me.

"Here!" he said. "The clerk gave it to me at the desk."

"Well, don't blame me!" I said.

I took the envelope, sat down heavily in the armchair by the window. I Pushed the curtain aside, and raised the blind.

It had been mailed from Buffalo, Miss Anthony's next stop. My hand trembled as I turned the envelope over. I knew what I would find. And there it was, black sealing wax.

"Blast!" I said. "Blast!"

"Go ahead, Millicent, open it," MacDuff said. He threw himself in the other armchair.

I broke the seal with my fingernail, removed the letter, and read:

"You can't fool me, MacDuff. You are a filthy Indian, your so-called assistant a black bitch with a little white blood. Miss Anthony, that nigger loving old wench who no doubt sleeps with that white haired slave Frederick Douglass, isn't fit to live, let alone cast a vote among God fearing gentlemen. Oh, and wasn't it just too awful about that poor old woman?"

I stuffed the letter back in the envelope. Then I stood up and threw the letter on the floor. I stamped on it, ground it under my heel. Had MacDuff not been there to stop me, I would have set a match to the obscenity and burned it in the grate.

"Evidence, Millicent," he said, quietly.

"MacDuff!" I screamed, "You must get the person who wrote that filth!" I gave the letter a kick, sending it skittering across the floor. "Whoever it is, you must get him!"

MacDuff picked up the obscenity, and after reading it, put his hands on my shoulders. He brought his face close to mine. His eyes glittered malevolently, his lips curled away from his teeth.

"You've got it wrong, Millicent. I won't get him. We will! Together, we'll get the inadv!" he said using the Cherokee word for snake. MacDuff looked like an animal ready to attack and kill.

As the train drew close to the city of Buffalo, we saw Lake Erie in the distance. There were dozens of steamships on the lake. Smoke curled up from the smokestacks. There were sailing vessels, too, three-mast monster relics of a dying age. Soot spewed from factory chimneys along the lakeshore.

The train sped through the countryside. Hedges, trees, bridges, and roads flashed by the window. The train hurtled through the Buffalo suburbs, its whistle screaming at crossings. The train slowed as we reached the city center, and kept slowing. We passed under bridges, crawled through hobo jungles.

Finally, the engine gave an ear-piercing scream. Steel wheels screeched, and sparks flew. Steam rolled the length of the train as we stopped next to the station platform. Looking out the window, I saw men from the Press running along the platform, one of them lugging a camera.

Helped down from the train by the porter, Miss Anthony was met by a brigade of stout matrons who formed a protective wall around her. Surrounded by her brigade, head held high, she strode through the depot to the brougham waiting in front of the station. The coachman opened the door and Miss Anthony, escorted by two of the largest and most buxom matrons, climbed inside.

The group of reporters crowded round the coach shouting questions. Miss Anthony looked out at them through the side window, smiling ever so slightly, until the matron closest to the window reached over and pulled up the shade. At that exact moment, the reporter with the camera lit the flash bar, and snapped a close-up shot of the closed window shade and the matron's pudgy fingers. Thinking, I suppose, of how much the photo would

110

impress his editor, the reporter cursed, then struck himself on the forehead with the heel of his hand.

Some of the reporters continued to crowd round until the driver, a large man with big shoulders and scowling brows, raised his whip and snapped the bowler hat off the head of the reporter standing nearest the coach. Then all the reporters stood back, and Miss Anthony and her protectors drove away.

I turned to look for MacDuff, but he was gone. Or so I thought.

"Here I am, Millicent."

I jumped possibly three feet above the platform. He was right behind me.

"MacDuff!" I hissed. "You scared me nearly out of my bloomers."

"Sorry, Millicent," he said, insincerely. He stared at me with his blue eye. "Millicent, while you were watching all those reporters did anything about the scene, I mean anything in particular, look a little odd?"

"What do you mean?"

"Well, I saw reporters waving notebooks," MacDuff said, "and one of them was toting a camera."

"Of course!"

MacDuff smiled.

"That there were reporters here at the station at all, was in itself most unusual," I said.

MacDuff nodded.

"There were no reporters to meet Miss Anthony at any of the other cities, not even Rochester, where she makes her home. So why were there so many reporters here?"

MacDuff removed a yellow circular from his pocket.

"Look." He handed the circular to me. "I peeled it off a pillar when we detrained."

It said, Mr. Frederick Douglas to Join Miss Susan B. Anthony at Speaking Engagement. Wednesday Afternoon, One O'clock P.M., Unitarian Universalist Church on Main Street.

"That's why that pack of newshounds showed up here

today," MacDuff said.

For thirty years the sensationalist press has bandied about the rumor that Miss Anthony and Mr. Douglass were romantically involved. The rumor was simply not true.

"So, MacDuff, now we know why Mr. Douglass's name was mentioned in the letter this morning. But why was the old woman mentioned?"

MacDuff scratched his chin.

"I don't know why the old woman was in the letter, Millicent. But I know that there could be a mean crowd in front of the church tomorrow on Main Street, carrying signs with unkind words, like those in the letters. I wouldn't be surprised if the K.K.K. showed up."

"You don't actually think the Ku Klux Klan would travel here all the way from Alabama, or Arkansas, or..."

"No, Millicent. You want to bet the Klan has a chapter right here in Buffalo?"

"Do you mean to say the Ku Klux Klan would dare show up in broad daylight wearing their bed sheets and pointy hats?"

MacDuff laughed. "They'll leave the sheets home, and the pointy hats too. Nevertheless, they might be there. Hate-filled stupid men whispering among themselves."

"Do you think they might do something awful, MacDuff?"

"They'll yell and shout, and make threats, but I don't think they'll do anything. At least, not the ones on the street. They'll be too visible. Besides, there'll be other men in the street too, men in blue helmets carrying revolvers and billy clubs...." MacDuff's voice trailed off.

"MacDuff?" I said. No response. I touched his arm. Nothing. He had gone to Palmer's Theater again. I watched his face for signs. A few minutes later he blinked, and cleared his throat.

"I'm worried, Millicent," he said. "Our would-be assassin could decide to create a disturbance. Maybe induce some K.K.K. members or a couple of Buffalo thugs to incite a riot, and then take advantage of the confusion. Like he did in Seneca Falls when he set that fire.

"But he won't be among the crowd in the street. No, he'll be hiding in a closed carriage hitched to a couple of fast horses, or up on a rooftop across the street from the Church."

"And everybody would be distracted, including the police."

"Correct, Millicent. Then at just the right moment…"

I shuddered. Another scary thought occurred to me.

"MacDuff! The assassin could kill them both, Miss Anthony and Mr. Douglass as well!"

"Yeah, he could make it two birds with one stone, Millicent; one black, and one white."

"MacDuff, the letter we received this morning hints at such a plan!"

In my imagination, I could see both Miss Anthony and Mr. Douglass shot dead upon the Unitarian Church steps.

"And, MacDuff, do you suppose the real plotters, the ones with the brains, would try to lay the blame at the door of the K.K.K.?"

"Maybe they'll try and make the K.K.K. the fall guys, but I don't think so. Anyhow, to us it really doesn't matter who takes the blame. Stopping the assassin from killing Miss Anthony or Mr. Douglass tomorrow, that's what matters.

"But we have to be prepared, Millicent. First thing is, we have to report this new development to Billy and Dixon. Where's Miss Anthony's staying?"

I removed the list from my shoulder bag.

"Here it is. Mrs. A.J. Harvey, wife of a prominent Buffalo factory owner. Address, 740 Delaware Avenue."

"If Miss Anthony is following the list Belle gave us, that'll be the place. And Billy and Dixon will already be there."

We asked the boy at the stable where we rented the carriage to recommended a hotel near the Harvey's Delaware Ave. address.

"Try the Nickel City Hotel," the boy said, "on Delaware Circle. It's jist round the corner from here, and only 'bout seven blocks from the Harvey residence."

MacDuff ran inside the Nickel City with our grips and booked our rooms, ran back out, jumped in the carriage, and off we went again. Reaching in his coat pocket, he pulled out a Buffalo map, which he handed to me.

"Take a look, Millicent. See if it shows any good places between our hotel and the Harvey residence, for an assassin to hide."

I studied the map. "MacDuff, the map shows a park that goes along Delaware Avenue to within a few blocks of the Harvey residence."

After about a block, I looked out the carriage window. "MacDuff, there it is." I pointed at the iron fence bordering the park on the left side of the street.

The Harvey mansion was on Delaware Avenue, at the corner of Park Place. It stood well back from the street, surrounded by a high iron fence topped with brass spikes. The façade was of white marble, the roof black slate with a central dome of gleaming copper.

"Some dive, huh, Millicent," MacDuff said. He slowed down the carriage.

Up the street about half a block beyond the Harvey mansion stood a delivery wagon missing its right-side back wheel. The axle rested on a block of wood. The wheel lay on the grass between the curb and the sidewalk. Next to the wheel stood a man in workman's clothes smoking a pipe.

"Guess who, Millicent?" MacDuff laughed.

"Who ever could it be?" I said.

We stopped behind the wagon. I put my hand to my breast. I raised an imaginary lorgnette and peered out at the man.

"Come here, my good man!" I called out.

Billy Bergin looked up. He removed his battered bowler and fussed with the brim.

"The lady said, come here!" MacDuff said.

Billy limped over to the carriage.

"How do you like my costume?" Billy kept his voice low.

Then he smiled, showing two blackened front teeth.

"I think it is wonderful, Billy," I said. "I especially like the gimpy right leg."

"Think I should try for a comeback, Millicent? I mean, if we ever go back to Old Broadway." Billy's eye twitched.

MacDuff rolled his eyes, shook his head. "We've got other things to talk about right now, Billy. Jump in."

Billy looked both ways up and down Delaware, then got in the carriage with us. MacDuff told Billy about Mr. Douglass. Billy snickered.

"Dixon and I already know about that, and guess what, MacDuff. Mr. Douglass is staying right here in the same house with her," Billy pointed. "Yep, right here at the Harvey joint, him and Miss Anthony."

Now it was my turn to roll my eyes. "Billy, I do hope the Press doesn't hear about that."

"If any reporters show up here, they'll be having to buy new equipment. They might even have to go visit a dentist. MacDuff." Billy's eye twitched. "MacDuff," Billy's eye twitched again. "Don't you think maybe we should call the cops in, just this one time?"

"I wish we could, Billy."

"MacDuff's right," I said. "Almost certainly, the press would hear about the plot, and Miss Anthony would..."

"Yeah, I know," Billy said. "She'd take it on the lam. MacDuff, there's something else you need to know."

"Okay, let's hear it, Billy."

"Dixon and I are sure we saw the assassin drive past where Miss Anthony stayed the night in Rochester."

MacDuff stiffened. "Was he alone?"

"Yeah, he was alone. The first time was just a little after dark. He drove past at a fast trot, then again about an hour later he drove by slow. It was the same coach and the same horse both times. After the second time, I sent Dixon to fetch a cab, and he went to your hotel. Dixon said you weren't there, so he left a note with the desk clerk."

"We never got the note," I said.

"The same coach came by again, around midnight. That

was the last time. MacDuff, he showed up at the farmhouse where she was staying in Albany. In fact, he would have made an attempt on Miss Anthony's life then if Dixon and I hadn't been there. We didn't see him near the Quaker family's house in Seneca Falls, but MacDuff, I think he'll show up here tonight."

MacDuff tilted his head back and studied the ceiling fabric. "Billy. I think all four of us had better stay close to the Harvey residence tonight."

Chapter 22

The Unitarian Universalist Church, built of rough-hewn reddish-brown stone adorned with a sooty patina of coal smoke, stood on North Main Street. Stone-cut steps led up to a set of enormous entrance doors. A sign on the doors said: "To See Minister, Go Around Back and Ring.'" We followed a brick sidewalk to the rear of the building, where a huge oak tree stood watch over a little graveyard. MacDuff twisted the key-shaped ringer on the door. We waited. MacDuff twisted the ringer again.

The door opened.

"Yes?"

He was a tall man with thinning hair.

"We're looking for…"

"I am Professor Smyth, minister of this church. Whom do I have the, uh, pleasure of addressing?"

"My name is MacDuff." He showed his P.I. license. "This is Miss Davies, my colleague."

"Please state your business."

"Our business is private."

Smyth started to speak again, but MacDuff sent a message with his blue eye that meant, "Better shut up, mister!"

Smyth shut up.

"We need to talk to you about something important," MacDuff said. "Make it someplace where not even the trees can overhear."

Smyth stepped aside and MacDuff and I went in. Smyth closed and locked the door. We followed him down a narrow hallway to a dimly lit study.

"Do sit down," Smyth said, indicating a matched set of leather armchairs facing his desk.

We sat. Smyth stood. Subdued light coming in through the window produced a halo effect round Smyth's head and shoulders. I stifled a laugh.

"What is it you want from me?" Smyth said, in a professorial tone.

I wanted to say, but did not, "Teacher, may I be excused, that I might go powder my nose?"

We told Professor Smyth our story, then told him we needed his cooperation. Also, we insisted that he repeat nothing we had shared with him to anyone, including the official police or the press, and we told him why. Professor Smyth sat down behind his desk. For the next several minutes, he said nothing. Then:

"You shall have my full cooperation." A different tone, a different person. "You have my word as an honorable man, and a clergyman: I shall not disclose what you have said to another living soul."

We got down to business. Smyth said the church held one hundred seventy-five people with all pews filled. For the event tomorrow afternoon, he expected a full house, and because Miss Anthony and Mr. Douglass, a white woman and a black man, would share the platform, Smyth said he had already requested assistance from the Buffalo Police Dept. Two armed policemen would be posted outside the church. More policemen would be available if needed.

MacDuff and I accompanied by Smyth went outside to assess how to keep the two famous speakers safe from an assassin's bullet when they stepped out of their coach, and walked up the steps to enter the church.

All buildings across the street from the church were privately owned houses. The buildings on either side of the church were also private dwellings, as were those that stood behind the church. It did not appear that an armed assassin could gain access to a window or a rooftop of one of those dwellings.

"Still," MacDuff said, "we'll keep an eye on windows and rooftops."

MacDuff explained, for Smyth's benefit, the security plan we would use.

"Dixon, one of our special deputies, will be out behind the church making sure nobody sneaks in at the back door. Billy, our other deputy, will circulate among the crowd on the street.

Millicent and I will be on either side of the church steps when Miss Anthony and Mr. Douglass arrive. Once we're all inside the church I'll take a seat in one of the back pews, on the aisle. Millicent will sit in the front row across from the lectern." MacDuff looked at Smyth.

"And if you don't mind taking an active role?"

"I should like to be of any assistance you deem fit, any at all," Smyth said.

"Your main job will be to take Miss Anthony and Mr. Douglass inside the church fast, after I take them from their coach up the steps to the door."

"Then they shall both arrive in the same coach?" Smyth said, incredulous.

"Probably, since they're both now staying at the same Delaware Avenue address."

"Oh my. That will raise an eyebrow or two." Smyth laughed quietly into his hand.

In the morning, I woke to the sound of pounding rain. I got up and raised the blind. Rain blew in sheets across the street below. Looking out over the rooftops, I saw Lake Erie in the distance. The lake and the sky were the same pewter gray.

I washed and dressed, and waited for MacDuff. I did not have long to wait. There was a knock on my door, and then came MacDuff's muffled voice speaking sweet nothings.

"Millicent! Aren't you up yet?"

I opened the door.

"We're in luck, Millicent!" He barged in, shutting the door behind him. "If the wind and rain keeps up like this, there won't be a mob at the church this afternoon."

MacDuff and I arrived at the church a few minutes before noon. The rain had not let up.

Smyth took us along the narrow passageway that led from the back exit, then out another door onto the stage that Miss Anthony and Mr. Douglass would soon share. The podium stood center stage, two chairs stood behind the podium. A set of steps led down from the stage. We followed Smyth down the steps, then up the center aisle to the back of the church, and then through a set of doors opening on the lobby. Smyth looked at his watch. It was time to open the doors.

Professor Smyth pushed open the main entrance doors, revealing a wonderfully dismal sight. It was still raining, in fact, much to our delight, it was raining even harder than before. MacDuff and I looked at each other, and smiled. No, an unruly mob had not gathered today on Main Street, and if the rain kept up a mob would not gather in the street later either.

Across from the church two helmeted policemen stood under a tree, each of them covered from neck to knees with a waterproof cape. Raindrops bounced off their blue helmets. The larger of the two policemen held a cigarette cupped in his hand. Smoke curled snake-like round his wrist.

MacDuff and I and Professor Smyth waited under the portico for the arrival of the coach that would bring Miss Anthony and Mr. Douglass to the church, and we waited for Billy Bergin and Dixon who would follow Miss Anthony and Mr. Douglass from the Harvey residence. To our surprise, Billy showed up first. Stopping the carriage a few doors past the church, he nodded to us as he got out and hitched the horse to a post.

The coach carrying Miss Anthony and Mr. Douglass arrived. His collar turned up and his hat pulled down to hide his face, MacDuff ran down the church steps and threw open the coach door. Miss Anthony stepped daintily down, opening her umbrella as her foot touched the sidewalk.

"Allow me, Miss Anthony," MacDuff said.

I watched Miss Anthony's face closely, and saw no indication that she recognized MacDuff.

MacDuff took Miss Anthony's arm and guided her quickly across the sidewalk and up the wide steps to the lobby entrance, where Professor Smyth took over. MacDuff then ran back to the carriage in time to help Mr. Douglass down and into the church.

Standing watching for trouble, I caught a glimpse of Dixon.

Having hitched his horse to a post, he hurried past me, and then ran down the brick sidewalk to guard the church backdoor.

As MacDuff had instructed, Professor Smyth led Miss Anthony and Mr. Douglass through the church, up onto the stage, then through the door at the back of the stage, and down the hall to his office. We thought it best for the two speakers to remain there until time for them to go to the platform.

Now the people began to arrive. Most of them came in expensive coaches. Four or five coaches arrived in a cluster. Coachmen helped ladies and gentlemen with umbrellas down from their coaches and into the church. These coaches drove off, and another flock arrived. Finally, the last coach arrived, wheels scraping the curb, and the last lady and gentleman got out and went into the church.

From our out-of-the-way place inside the lobby, MacDuff and I looked closely at each person who came in, mostly women of course. Then it was time for us to go in and claim our seats.

The church was not quite full. There were, I guessed, about twenty-five vacant seats, most of them in the back pews. However, just minutes before Professor Smyth introduced the famous speakers, some latecomers filed in. I deduced that they had come by horse car, for their clothes were wet. Plainly dressed, they wore no expensive hats or precious stones. Some of them wore kerchiefs on their heads. Immigrants and the daughters of immigrants. Garment workers from the nearby mills.

As a sort of prelude, Miss Anthony had this to say to her audience. MacDuff and I recognized it for what it was, and were somewhat taken aback.

"There is, I think, a gentleman (I use that term loosely) among us today who would try to frighten me away from what I believe to be the true purpose of my life. I would say to this man, do not for a minute think me utterly stupid for failing to heed his warning. For there is another man among us today, along with a woman, his dear brave partner, who have made it their mission to protect me. I have complete faith that they will succeed."

MacDuff and I found this introduction to Miss Anthony's actual speech, a rather disconcerting message.

I was thrilled by Miss Anthony's speech, as would any woman be who believed in Suffrage. But I thought I would burst with African pride when Miss Anthony sat down, and Mr. Frederick Douglass strode to the lectern and delivered his powerful message. I found it almost impossible to take my eyes from his handsome face.

When Mr. Douglass finished, he walked over and took Miss Anthony's hand. Her tiny white hand disappeared in Mr. Douglass's large black hand. They walked to the front of the platform. They smiled at each other, the African King of Equal Rights and the Dowager Queen of Women's Suffrage. Mr. Douglass and Miss Anthony faced the audience, and bowed.

Then the little group of women who had come late, stood up as one from the back pews, and began the applause. They clapped their bare immigrant hands, coarsened by work in the mills. Some of the fine women wearing gloves, just a few of them at first, the braver souls among them, threw off their gloves and stood up. Joining the working women in their midst, they, too, clapped barehanded. Then more gloves came off. Soon all the women in the church were on their feet, and the few men among them as well. The sustained applause shook the church rafters.

Before the applause subsided, I saw Professor Smyth lead Miss Anthony and Mr. Douglass through the door at the back of the platform. As planned, Smyth would stay with them in his study until the church emptied out.

The people filed out of the church onto the street, and coaches came and carried them away. MacDuff and I stood out of sight in the church lobby, watching.

By then, the rain had stopped. The group of mill workers stood on the sidewalk near the church steps. They had formed a little circle around a woman whom I recognized at once, though she stood with her back to me. Mabel Singer. MacDuff saw her too.

"Well, well," he said. "There she is, the Mother of Birth Control. I knew she'd be here today breaking the Comstock Laws."

As I hurried down the church steps, I thought of Anthony Comstock, who founded the Society for the Suppression of Vice and once boasted that he had burned thousands of books, including books by Walt Whitman, Leo Tolstoy and George Bernard Shaw, because he thought them obscene.

But before I could reach Mabel Singer she had handed out the last of her pamphlets, climbed in a waiting coach and drove away. As in Poughkeepsie, I was sure that I saw a man's face watching out the rear window of the coach.

I raced up the steps to rejoin MacDuff.

"MacDuff, here come Miss Anthony and Mr. Douglass," I said, out of breath.

They had come from Professor Smythe's office and were now in the lobby ready to leave.

"And here comes the Harvey family coach to collect them," MacDuff said.

MacDuff and I ran to our carriage. The Harvey coach, with Miss Anthony and Mr. Douglass on board, went down Main to the next corner, then turned. From behind us, I heard the noisy clatter of another coach, then another. First Billy sped past hell-bent in his hansom cab, and then along came Dixon. They followed the Harvey family coach around the corner, Billy leaning hard to the inside to keep his two-wheeler from tipping over.

"We made good choices in those two young men," I said.

"And thanks to the weather, Millicent, bad things that could've happened, didn't."

"I was never so glad to see it rain so hard!"

Chapter 23

An hour after darkness fell, we drove up Delaware Avenue toward the Harvey residence. As we passed Dixon's coach near the Harvey front entrance, Dixon touched the brim of his hat. That meant Miss Anthony and Mr. Douglass were in the house, and that the coast was, now, clear of assassins. MacDuff turned the cab around on the wide avenue and stopped at the curb about half a block behind Dixon's coach.

It turned out to be a long and tiresome vigil. And while we waited, the night grew cooler and light fog fell around us. Around midnight, finally, a coach drove slowly toward us from downtown. It was hard to see the driver in the fog. There did not appear to be anyone inside the coach. The coach passed us, continued up the street a block, or so, then came back again. It went on by, and when the coach lights disappeared in the thickening fog, MacDuff touched our horse on the rump with the whip, and we followed. We came upon the coach, suddenly. It had stopped at the curb, under a streetlamp, and the driver seemed to have disappeared.

MacDuff pulled our coach to the curb and stopped. We could hear footsteps ahead of us, close by, but could not see the person who was walking down the street. We got out of the coach, crossed over the sidewalk on tiptoe, and ran along the strip of grass that bordered the cut stones, thinking we would catch up. Then the sound of the footsteps ceased.

"Oh, oh." I said.

Standing still, we strained to hear. Then we heard them again! Now the sound came from somewhere behind us, and were moving rapidly towards us. Whoever it was had doubled back, somehow. MacDuff reached inside his coat and drew out his revolver. I removed my Iver Johnson from my shoulder bag. Who was it? Where had he come from? Maybe from inside Delaware Park. Maybe he had climbed the fence. We returned to the sidewalk.

"Let's just keep walking," MacDuff said, "as though we heard nothing."

The footsteps grew near. A huge tree loomed at the sidewalk's edge. We ducked quickly behind the tree. The footsteps slowed, then abruptly stopped.

In the near distance, another sound! A horse and carriage moving slowly down the cobblestones. Clippety-clop, clippety-clop along the street in the fog. Billy and Dixon in their coach, I hoped.

Footsteps again! Moving faster now along the sidewalk. MacDuff and I stayed close to our tree, guns drawn, waiting to see who it was, and ready to jump out at him. Ready, if necessary, to shoot!

My eyes burned straining to see through the fog. A dark shape gradually emerged, the shadowy figure of a man! Now walking soundlessly, he continued toward us.

When he was within ten yards of us, MacDuff and I jumped out from our hiding place behind the tree, with our guns aimed at the shadowy figure. Seeing us and seeing the guns, he leaped across the narrow strip of grass next to the sidewalk and bounded into the street. The man raced across the wide street, then ran down the sidewalk on the other side of Delaware towards the river. MacDuff ran after him. Then from the direction of the Harvey residence a coach came upon us. Billy Bergin in our hansom! It came to a stop. Still running hard, footsteps echoing in the distance, the man disappeared in the fog.

"MacDuff! I yelled. "It's Billy with our hansom, come back!"

MacDuff came running across Delaware, out of breath.

"I left Dixon to watch the Harvey residence, in case the assassin doubles back, or one of his agents, if he's got one, shows up there!"

"Good job, Billy!" MacDuff shouted. "Now we've got to catch that guy. You, Billy, jump on the back of the hansom!"

Billy did. MacDuff and I climbed up on the seat. MacDuff slapped the horse on the neck with the reins, and away we flew.

"Blast this bloody fog!" I yelled.

"Millicent, our man's heading toward the river, and you can bet there'll be a launch waiting for him there to take him to

Canada. We have to stop him before he gets to the river!"

Our man, as MacDuff called him, was invisible. MacDuff drove through the fog like a madman, the two-wheeler bouncing and swaying down the middle of the street.

"Where did you learn to drive with such reckless daring?" I shouted. The coach made an awful racket on the cobblestones. Holding onto the strap with both hands, I thought of poor Billy hanging on for dear life on the back of the hansom.

"On Blackwell's Island." MacDuff spoke in a staccato rhythm as he drove like a madman down the street. "I was a trustee. I transported sick prisoners to the infirmary!"

"My god, MacDuff! How many did you scare to death on the way?"

Soon, we came upon the assassin. Pulling back on the reins with one hand to slow down the hansom, with his other hand MacDuff took aim at the fleeing man.

"Stop where you are!" MacDuff shouted.

At that spot, a narrow alleyway met the street. The alleyway was too narrow for a cab but wide enough for a man on foot. The man we chased darted into the alleyway, and vanished before MacDuff could bring the hansom to a stop.

"At the end of that alley, there's a service road that runs parallel to Delaware Avenue, that goes all the way to Delaware Circle," MacDuff shouted. "I saw it when I studied the map!"

Suddenly, out of the pitch dark at the end of the alley came a bright red/orange flash, and a simultaneous explosion. The bullet tore through the side of the hansom, and struck the brick wall of a building the other side of Delaware Avenue. Someone opened a window.

"What the hell's going on?" cried a voice.

"You want me to chase him down that alley, MacDuff?" Billy shouted.

"No!" MacDuff yelled. "We'll need you later, at the river."

We lurched away from the curb. Anticipating the gunman's next move, MacDuff drove to the corner half a block away. We nearly tipped over going round the corner. For a frightening moment, one wheel rose up from the cobblestones. Billy cursed.

"There he is, Millicent!" MacDuff shouted a moment later.

I saw a coach fly out of the service road that ran behind the buildings fronting Delaware Avenue. The coach sped across our path. Sparks from the horse's hooves danced on the paving stones.

"He must have had a coach hidden in the service road by prearrangement, MacDuff!" I yelled over the clatter of carriage wheels.

"Right, Millicent!"

MacDuff followed the coach round the next corner. We drove and drove through a labyrinth of narrow streets and alleys until the poor horse was in a lather and my nerves were near the end of their tether.

On we went, losing sight of the coach one minute, catching sight of it again the next. Fortunately, the hour was late, so traffic was light, and the few coaches we met gave the assassin, and the three crazy people chasing him, a wide berth.

Most of the streets down which we flew ran parallel to Delaware Avenue. Then at Delaware Circle, near the Nickel City Hotel, again MacDuff nearly tipped the hansom over when our quarry veered round a corner and headed toward the river.

Before we could catch up, the assassin reached one of the piers at the water's edge.

MacDuff brought the hansom to a skidding halt behind the abandoned coach, and leaped onto the quay. But we were too late. The assassin had already jumped aboard the launch, which had been waiting with full steam up. We watched the trim and speedy craft fly quickly out of sight on the river in the fog.

"Can you live without this?" MacDuff said to Billy, meaning Billy's hat.

"Sure," Billy shrugged.

Snatching Billy's hat off his head, MacDuff crushed it into something unrecognizable, and then threw it in the river. We watched the current carry it away.

As we got back in the hansom, Billy squeezed inside with us. Never before had I sat so close to MacDuff.

"Ummm, nice," I said.

"What?" MacDuff said.

Billy stifled a laugh with his hand.

On the way to the hotel, we spoke of the events of the night.

"He thought of everything, everything, right from the start!" MacDuff said. "And I misjudged him, underestimated him. That was stupid!"

"He arranged to have a coach waiting in the alley. Arranged in advance to have that steam launch ready and waiting at the pier, not because he knew he'd have a chance to kill Miss Anthony today, and maybe Mr. Douglass too. No, he arranged to have that launch ready just in case he stumbled on an opportunity. If he had killed Miss Anthony or Mr. Douglass, or both of them, the launch would've given him another means of escape. He wouldn't have to rely only on the trains, and wouldn't have to hire a special, and wouldn't have to chance making his getaway in a carriage. He could've jumped aboard the launch, and been in Canada in fifteen minutes! Which is what he just did."

MacDuff grew quiet.

"But who was the man we chased all the way across Buffalo, MacDuff? None of us ever had a good look at him. The blasted fog!"

"I'd like to know who was in that boat that was waiting for him at the pier," said Billy Bergin.

"Well, at least now we know with certainty that the assassin is not working alone," I said.

Back at the Nickel City Hotel, we piled out of the hansom. Billy went to rejoin Dixon at the Harvey residence.

It had been a long day. MacDuff and I went to my room and smoked a cigarette, and tried to shake off some of the tension. MacDuff got up. He crushed his cigarette out in the ashtray and started out the door to go to his room. He stopped in the hallway, just outside the door.

"Millicent," he said. "Back there when the assassin shot at

us from that alley, and the bullet slammed through the hansom only inches from your head..."

I came out in the hallway and stood next to him.

MacDuff rested his hand on my shoulder. Then, his voice a whisper, he said, "Millicent, you could've been killed." He looked down at his boots. "Except for that…"

"Yes, Boss?" I said

He looked into my eyes, and then quickly looked away.

"Well?"

"I can't think of anyone I'd rather have had with me tonight!"

MacDuff dashed inside his room, and slammed the door.

"Thanks, MacDuff," I said to the closed door. Then, in a whisper, "'…may flights of angels sing thee to thy rest…'"

Chapter 24

There was no letter waiting for us at the front desk this time when we checked out. But the absence of another of those hateful letters left me feeling neither reassured, nor hopeful.

We purchased our tickets at the depot; then we joined the scores of other people, most of them women, who milled about on the platform.

"And to think that all of these people are probably going to Lily Dale," I said to MacDuff as we stood and waited for Miss Anthony to arrive.

I pointed to a handbill on a post. It said, "Special Excursions to Lily Dale to Celebrate Women's Day Events, August 14 and 15." It listed one train, ours, leaving for Lily Dale this morning, two leaving in the afternoon, then two more excursions leaving the next morning.

"Be right back." MacDuff said, abruptly.

The Western Union Office was next to the ticket window. I assumed MacDuff had gone in to see whether we had messages.

He came back out with an envelope.

"I sent a wire from Rochester to an old professor at NYU."

MacDuff opened the envelope. "Remember?"

I nodded. MacDuff read the message silently. His eyes narrowed. He folded the message back into the yellow envelope, and slipped it in his pocket.

"Well?" I said, curious, "what did the professor have to say? And, incidentally, why did you wire the old man in the first place?"

"I'll tell you later, Millicent." He didn't. Not for some time.

Just then, a Western Union messenger boy came running out of the office.

"Message for Mr. MacDuff! Message for Mr. MacDuff!" he shouted.

"Over here!" MacDuff waved at the boy.

MacDuff accepted the envelope, and dropped a dime in

the boy's hand. The boy said, "Thanks." and turned to leave.

"Wait a minute, young man," MacDuff said, catching him by the arm. "This is no telegram, it's a letter."

"Yes, sir," the boy said. "A man brought it in our office just a few minutes ago. He said it's for a gentleman out on the platform, and then he said your name, and then he gave me twenty-five cents and said go deliver this message to you. He said jist yell yer name."

"Where is this man now?" MacDuff said.

"Oh, I saw him go git in a big shiny coach and drive away, and he was drivin' plenty fast too."

MacDuff showed the boy a silver dollar, the boy gulped.

"Describe the man," MacDuff said.

After some stuttering and stammering, the boy described a man who, in general, matched up with Billy Bergin's description of Brian Donovan, one of our suspects.

"About six feet tall, he was, and kinda well dressed. Hair sorta yellow, sorta long," the boy said.

"It does sound like Donovan," I said.

"He could be the man hired to pull the trigger. But the letters, how could a lug like him write them?"

"Maybe somebody else wrote the letters, MacDuff, and Donovan, as you say, is just the stooge with the gun?"

"Maybe." He handed me the envelope.

I studied it closely. Nothing was typed on the envelope, but a brief glance at the back revealed that it was from him alright.

"Let's wait to read it till we're on the train, Millicent," MacDuff said.

I stuffed the envelope in my bag.

Miss Anthony was among the first passengers to board the train to Lily Dale. MacDuff and I, on this occasion posing as a married couple, got on soon after. We sat, together this time, four rows behind Miss Anthony who occupied an aisle seat near the front of the car. Soon all seats were taken.

Billy and Dixon, posing as businessmen, were in the car

behind ours. About every fifteen minutes, one of them walked through our car, and into the cars ahead, then back through ours again. On one occasion, they walked through together, talking, too loudly at times, about stocks and bonds. The club car being ahead of ours gave our agents a good excuse for walking through our car so frequently.

After we were well underway, I opened my bag and retrieved the letter. I felt sick to my stomach even before breaking the seal. I read the filthy thing to myself.

> *"Good morning,"* it began. *"My, what an adventure last night turned out to be, Mr. MacDuff. And what a consummate actress your little Negress whore turned out to be. I must admit, you and she had me fooled for a moment. I shall keep a closer watch from now on, as our interesting little production moves toward the final curtain. What next -- high opera?"*

I was so angry. I could not scream, so instead I wept. Quietly, so that no one but MacDuff would know. I shoved the message into MacDuff's hand, and he read it. Then I sat up straight, my back barely touching the upholstery, my head aligned perfectly upon my squared shoulders, chin tilted slightly upward, in that perfectly balanced posture expected of all Victorian ladies, even Free Thinkers and Suffragists, and Bohemians like me.

MacDuff gave the letter back to me. He leaned against the firm seat.

"Millicent," he said. "Give me a nice big jewelry heist or a murder case any day. Give me a crime with a victim, and a thief or a murderer to catch."

I put the letter in my bag with the other obscene missives. Then I raised my window to let in fresh air.

Chapter 25

The train stopped a dozen times on the way to Lily Dale to take on more passengers, and stopped once, briefly, to hook on two more passenger cars. There had to have been five hundred people on board, when the train chugged into the Lily Dale depot at half past one in the afternoon. Standing in the aisle waiting to detrain, MacDuff and I looked out the window and saw Billy and Dixon following Miss Anthony along the crowded platform. A porter pushing a cart laden with luggage forged ahead.

A coach was there to meet Miss Anthony, who was carrying her famous alligator purse. She kept it with her always, never left it unattended, and would not allow anyone to carry it for her. The porter helped her into the coach, and then put her things on the luggage rack in back. Billy and Dixon followed the slow moving four-wheeler on foot, carrying their grips.

MacDuff and I hauled our grips to one of the dozen commercial freight wagons that were there to meet the train. The driver carted MacDuff and me, along with a dozen other travelers and their luggage, across a wooden bridge that spanned a narrow channel. The channel connected the last two of three lakes called, collectively, the Cassadaga Lakes. Lily Dale hugged the north shore of the third lake, which was the largest of the three. The horses clomped noisily. The wagon creaked, the wheels rumbled, the water flowed silently under the bridge.

The driver, a thin young man with jowls, brought our wagon to a stop at the entrance to the Lily Dale grounds. The ornate sign curving over the gate said, Cassadaga Lakes Free Association. A white-bearded man stood at the gate with a smile on his face and his hand out. All of us on the wagon paid the ten-cent daily fee, the young man with jowls flicked the reins, and the team hauled us onto the grounds. The horses drew our wagon down Cleveland Drive, a narrow dirt road that curved around a little park. Turning off Cleveland Drive, the wagon rolled to a stop at the entrance to the Grand Hotel. The hotel stood among many stately old Maple trees.

The driver gave us instructions. You had to listen closely, because when he spoke it was a baffling mumbo jumbo that sounded like water running down a sluice.

"Whatever did he say?" whispered a bonneted woman seated next to me on the wagon.

"According to the young man," I said, grinning, "we must 'go up them there steps.' He says the hotel desk is through 'that there door yonder.'"

The young man pointed at the door with his chin. A rivulet of tobacco juice trickled out the corner of his wide mouth, then down onto his chin where he caught it, deftly, with the sleeve of his shirt. Three boys came out and carried all the luggage inside the lobby. MacDuff and I, and the other passengers, followed the boys inside.

When it came our turn to register, MacDuff and I stepped up to the desk. A sign said Mr. Rouse, Manager. Behind the sign stood a barrel-shaped red-faced man with handlebar mustaches. He gave a hearty 'welcome!' and opened the hotel register.

"And how long will you and, uh, the Mrs. be staying with us, sir?" said Mr. Rouse. He gave a little cough behind his hand. MacDuff nodded to me.

"He is Mr. Joseph Bell, of Philadelphia, PA," I lied. "I am his associate Miss Wells, also of Philadelphia. We are here from our newspaper the *Philadelphia Guardian* to cover the Woman's Day festivities. We wired ahead two days ago, asking for rooms close together. 'On the first floor, if possible,' we specified in our wire."

I gave the manager my sweetest, most innocent smile.

"Very good, uh, Miss Wells. Yes, of course." Mr. Rouse reddened. He consulted his room list.

"Oh, but I am sorry to say we had but three rooms vacant when we received your wire." He studied the register further. "Ah! I see there were two adjoining rooms, on the third floor, which were reserved for you. I do hope…"

"That'll be fine," MacDuff interrupted. "We'll take them."

"Very good, sir. That will be rooms 331 and 333." He pointed at the stairs, to the right of the desk. "Turn left at the top of the stairs. Your rooms will be on the right hand side of the hallway."

MacDuff removed his wallet from an inside pocket.

"How much?"

"You say you'll be staying how many nights?"

"Three."

"That will be $4.50, in advance, sir."

MacDuff paid, and handed me the receipt. We signed the register with our fictitious names, and Mr. Rouse handed us our keys.

Turning to leave, MacDuff saw a pile of maps on the desk showing all the streets and sites of Lily Dale. The sign said Free. MacDuff took two of the maps, handing one to me to stuff into my already over-stuffed shoulder bag.

MacDuff and I carried our own grips to the Third Floor and deposited them in our respective rooms.

Soon after, the maid showed up with fresh water and clean towels. I closed the door to my room and washed the dust from my face. A few minutes later, MacDuff knocked at our adjoining door. I opened it.

"We have to go find Billy and Dixon," he said, "and then find the Lassing-Tilton residence. According to our list, it's where Miss Anthony's staying."

We walked down the stairs to the lobby, and were about to step out onto the hotel porch.

"Hey, you two."

It was Billy Bergin, sitting back in the corner of the lobby next to a window. We exchanged greetings, then left the hotel lobby. We crossed the porch, and then went down the steps into the park where we found a bench to sit on under the trees.

"The home of Miss Anthony's friend is near the entrance, second house from the gate, as you come in, on the right-hand side of Melrose Park. Dixon and I saw her go in. On the porch post, it says number Five. I got a bed at a rooming house right next door. Dixon rented a room on Cottage Row, the street that runs along the other side of the park."

"Good work, Billy," MacDuff said.

"Got anything important for me and Dixon?"

MacDuff told him about the assassin's latest letter.

"First thing is, Millicent and I have to find out where in the village Miss Anthony will do her speech. Then we can check to see what kind of security problems we're facing. Once we finish that part of our investigation, we can start making a plan that'll keep Miss Anthony alive. We'll need your take on that, and Dixon's too."

"Okay. Right now Dixon's trying to watch both the front and back of the Lassing-Tilton house, so I can't sit here gabbing with you two much longer."

Billy stood up. MacDuff caught his arm.

"He's here already, Billy."

"You've seen him?"

"No, but he's here alright. Bet on it."

"Dixon and I will keep our eyes open, MacDuff," he said, and started to leave. He stopped mid-stride, turned around and said:

"MacDuff, I sure do wish Miss Anthony would do her speech tomorrow instead of the day after." Billy's eye twitched.

"I know, Billy. It worries hell out of me and Millicent too."

"I just hope Miss Anthony stays put at her friend's house tomorrow, and doesn't go walking around all day long making a target out of herself."

Billy left. MacDuff and I walked around the hotel to Melrose Park, where we found the Auditorium. A large building with whitewashed walls, it stood at the north end of the Park, a short walk from the hotel. A handbill tacked to the side of the building near the main entrance door said:

Special Event!
Susan B. Anthony to Speak on Woman's Suffrage.
August 15. Two thirty in the afternoon.
Lily Dale Auditorium.

"This is the place alright," MacDuff said. "Now we need to look inside."

We found a grounds keeper cutting grass in another little park between the auditorium and the Grand Hotel. MacDuff gave the old man the usual story. "We're news reporters…" Etcetera.

"We really must have a look inside," MacDuff said. "Otherwise, my good man, we shall not know the best place to set up our photography equipment."

"You young folks just follow me," the grounds keeper said.

We followed him to the auditorium main entrance, where he selected one of many keys he carried on a ring tied to his belt, and unlocked the door.

"Bring me the key when you're done," the groundskeeper said.

The auditorium interior was nearly square. The main entrance door was on the south wall of the building. There was an exit door at the other end of the same wall, another exit at the north side of the building, directly across from the main entrance. The stage ran along the east wall, at the front of the place. Gaslights hung from the high ceiling.

Climbing up the stairs onto the stage, we discovered one more door, the stage door. That door was hidden from the audience behind blue floor-to-ceiling curtains, which ran along the stage about a third of its length.

I looked at MacDuff. His eyes were glazed, and out of focus. He spoke so quietly, I could barely hear his words.

"Billy and Dixon will be outside," MacDuff began. "They'll watch the stage door, and the exit door across from the main entrance. We'll watch all the other doors from our positions inside. I'll be standing at about the center of that raised platform that runs along the south wall. Over there." MacDuff indicated the spot with a nod of his head.

"Millicent, you'll be directly across from me." He pointed at the raised platform that went along the north wall. "You'll position yourself about center of the platform, near that other exit door."

I nodded.

MacDuff was making observations and setting a scene. We stood at about the center of the auditorium, facing the stage, as he described what he saw with his mind's eye.

"Our positions across from each other on those raised

platforms will allow us to see over everybody's head, and see everything happening up on the stage as well."

He paused. I looked at his face. It was a grim angry face, I thought. But his eyes had come back into focus. He was back in my world again.

MacDuff shook his head. "Yeah, Millicent. All we have to do is watch all the doors, and at the same time watch all the people in the audience, and then pick out which of the three or four thousand people in the joint is the assassin."

MacDuff's jaws were set, his brown eye shut. A pinpoint of light shone in his blue eye, as it often did, like bright sunlight on gunmetal.

"Millicent," he said. "Over the years working for The Blind Lady I've been in some tight spots. But this?"

MacDuff shrugged. "Let's go find some place to eat."

We settled for hotdogs at a stand in the park next to Cottage Row, at the south side of the auditorium. We sat on a bench under an oak tree and ate our hotdogs, washing them down with iced tea. The hotdogs reminded me of sweltering Coney Island summer days when Lower Manhattan was unbearable.

We finished our lunch, such as it was.

"Millicent," MacDuff said, "let's go back to the Grand Hotel porch and try out those wicker rocking chairs."

I gave him a questioning look.

"Other than Justus Schwab's Saloon, can you think of any place we'd be more likely to hear something that could help us in our investigation? Who knows, Millicent," he laughed his meager Indian laugh. "Maybe we'll catch the assassin gossiping about the plot with some corseted old matron."

I had to agree with MacDuff about the Grand Hotel porch. To people who had been coming regularly to Lily Dale, I later learned, it was known simply as The Porch. And MacDuff was right. It was a lot like Justus Schwab's Saloon, except there were no loud drunken men cursing each other in seven different languages. People met on The Porch to talk about any topic you could imagine. They talked about religion, mostly Spiritualism, of course. Also, politics and philosophy, automatic writing and literature, history and mesmerism. The list goes on.

We walked from our bench near the hotdog vender to the Grand Hotel, and up onto the porch. White wicker rocking chairs lined the wide porch floor. Most of the chairs were unoccupied. MacDuff and I sat down in side-by-side rockers near the hotel main entrance. Two women sitting nearby were talking about Red Indian Spirit Guides, not a topic, I thought, exactly related to our case.

Aside from an occasional twittering of birds, or the soft snorting of horses passing in the unpaved streets, there were no intrusive sounds. What a delightful contrast, I mused sleepily, to the cacophony MacDuff and I endured every day in our second story consulting rooms. All day, every day horse's hooves pounded the cobblestones and rattled our windows. Even with our windows closed, we could not shut out the angry shouts and curses of the men who drove the wagons.

Rather abruptly, I became once again aware of my surroundings. I opened my eyes and saw that many rocking chairs were now in use. Soon more people arrived, to rock and relax. Some came out onto the porch from the hotel lobby. Perhaps they had had afternoon tea in the dining room. I looked over at MacDuff, who had his eyes closed. I leaned close.

"Are you asleep, MacDuff?" I said quietly.

He opened one eye, the blue one. He looked around. He yawned.

"Where is everybody Millicent, where are all the people? Judging from what we've seen of the grounds today, there's no where near three thousand people walking around Lily Dale."

MacDuff was right. Although we had seen many people on the grounds since our arrival, the numbers fell far short of the thousands expected in Lily Dale for Miss Anthony's speech.

"But Miss Anthony is not scheduled to speak till Sunday afternoon, two days from now," I said. "Probably most people will not arrive till tomorrow, possibly not until Sunday morning."

MacDuff had seemed preoccupied. Then he whispered:

"Millicent, I meant what I said to Billy earlier today. The assassin is here."

Something in his tone made me shiver.

"Yes, I feel it too."

"He might be right here. I mean in the hotel."

I shivered again.

I leaned against the cushioned back of my rocker, relishing the comfort.

"This little village is so deliciously quiet, MacDuff," I said.

"Too damned quiet, Millicent."

I knew what he meant. As the day for Miss Anthony's speech drew nearer our tension rose higher. I felt certain the assassin would attempt to kill Miss Anthony right here in Lily Dale. Perhaps during Miss Anthony's speech on Sunday, when all eyes were upon her. While three or four thousand admirers sat in rapt silence, hanging on Miss Anthony's every word, a shot would ring out.

That was one possibility. Or maybe the assassin would wait till after the speech. Perhaps in the middle of the night, when everyone in the village was asleep, a gunshot would shatter the silence.

Chapter 26

We left the Grand Hotel porch and walked along Cleveland Drive toward the Lily Dale beach. We followed a footpath that went along the lakeshore, in places but a few yards from the water's edge. A Weeping Willow tree standing between the path and the lake, reminded me of an old woman I once saw in a tenement house courtyard, bent over a rain barrel washing her hair.

A two-story frame building stood on the beach. The Bunch Club, which had a bowling alley on the first floor, a billiards parlor on the second. Next door to the Bunch Club was a bathhouse where for a nickel, according to the sign, you could take a refreshing hot bath any time of the day or night. MacDuff went in the men's side; I walked in and out of the women's side.

"No one in there looked like an assassin," I said to MacDuff outside.

MacDuff agreed. And we saw no one of interest in the Bunch Club.

Continuing our stroll, we walked up and down all the dusty side streets that ran from Cleveland Drive along the lake to East Street at the top of the hill. Ending up half an hour later back at the Grand Hotel, we plopped down on the porch, to rock and rest.

Billy Bergin showed up. We had seen him sitting on a bench in Melrose Park on our way back to the hotel. MacDuff had given him a nod that meant 'follow us, at a distance.' Billy stood leaning on the porch railing.

"She's safe," he said. "Hasn't left the house at all."

"See anybody of interest hanging around the house, or in the park?" MacDuff said.

"Nobody."

"Where is Dixon?" I said.

"Watching the house where Miss Anthony's staying," Billy said. "He's trying to watch both the front and back doors again, so I have to go back there right now."

Billy walked quickly down the porch steps and headed to Melrose Park.

It was nearly eight o'clock when we entered Byron's Café on Cleveland Drive. There was no one in the place except a thickset man standing behind the counter with a cigar in his mouth. Byron, no doubt. Something told me it was a little late in the evening to order dinner. Byron had his hands on his hips and a scowl on his face. His demeanor seemed to say, "Go ahead, order something. I dare you."

The cook stove stood against the back wall. Something simmered in a big pot at the back of the stovetop.

"What's that?" MacDuff pointed at the pot.

"Chicken and bean stew," Byron rasped.

"I'll take a chance on the stew," MacDuff said.

"So shall I," I said.

Byron loaded large portions onto oval dinner plates.

"Youse want bread, too?"

MacDuff looked at me. I nodded.

"Sure," MacDuff said.

Byron sawed two thick slices from the loaf on the sideboard. He slathered the bread with butter, and set the bread on our plates atop the chicken and beans.

"Would youse like coffee?"

We nodded. Byron filled two mugs from a steaming pot.

"The coffee's kinda old, and maybe pretty strong," he said.

Byron brought the stew and coffee to our table. Staring at our mounded plates, we bent to the task. It was a lot of chicken and beans, and surprisingly tasty. MacDuff mopped his plate hobo style. We did not finish our coffee. MacDuff left fifty cents on the table to cover the meal, and folded a Morgan greenback under his plate to make friends with Byron.

Chapter 27

The map MacDuff picked up at the hotel showed not only all the streets of Lily Dale, it also indicated walking paths that wound through the two-hundred acres of woods surrounding the village. Leaving the café, we strolled up First Street. At the top of First Street stood a picnic pavilion next to a field, and across the field was a woods.

"A potential escape route for an assassin, or a good place to hide," I said, looking at the line of trees along the edge of the field.

We walked through the pavilion and across the field, where we found a path leading into the woods. We followed the path a hundred yards, or so, then retraced our steps.

We sat down at a table in the pavilion and studied the details of our map. The path we had followed into the woods curved to the right, according to the map, coming out, finally, by the horse barns on South Street at the other end of the village.

"Look here, Millicent," MacDuff said, studying our map. "The map shows what looks like a big pond or a small lake dotted with little islands." MacDuff pointed to the place on the map. "Beyond the pond, there's a road. Looks like the road takes you to that town we came through on the train. Fredonia, wasn't it?"

"Yes. I think so, MacDuff."

We left the pavilion and walked to South Street, where we found another woods with another path. We followed this path till we came to a sign nailed to a post. It said, "Inspiration Stump." Known locally simply as The Stump, it is all that remains of a giant Maple tree, and was a sort of shrine. Rows of benches faced The Stump.

When we left the strange little shrine in the woods, it had grown dark.

"Time to go find Billy and Dixon, to hear their evening report" MacDuff said.

"Time for me to go back to the hotel to freshen up. I am tired, MacDuff."

We walked back to the pavilion, then down First Street

together. Gaslights shone from parlor windows. Insects buzzed round us. People passed, the women nodding, the men touching their hat brims. At the bottom of First Street, where it met Cleveland Drive, we parted.

"See you at the hotel in half an hour, Millicent. On the porch."

MacDuff went along the wide path behind the hotel toward Melrose Park to find Billy and Dixon. I crossed Cleveland Drive, climbed the steps onto the hotel porch, and went up to my room.

I washed up quickly, then lay down to rest.

I woke with a start. MacDuff was knocking on the adjoining door, and calling my name. I bounded off the bed, straightened my clothes and opened the door.

"I fell asleep, MacDuff," I said embarrassed.

"I thought so, when I didn't find you on the porch."

"What did Billy and Dixon have to report?" I yawned.

"There's nothing interesting going on in Melrose Park."

By now, we were both all in, and knew what we must face in the morning. Somehow MacDuff and I, and our agents, had to keep Miss Anthony alive. To me it seemed an overwhelming task. In fact, I thought it might prove impossible.

We bade each other goodnight. MacDuff went through the adjoining door to his room. I got into my nightdress and threw on my robe. I lit the lamp on the table next to the armchair, and curled up and wrote in my journal. Through our connecting door, I heard MacDuff singing. I did not understand the words, because they were in Cherokee. He had been doing ceremony, as he called it. He was consulting The Blind Lady using Grandfather's Pipe. The song was what he sang to end the ceremony, a sort of amen, he once said.

I felt a draft on my shoulder. Marking my place, I closed my journal and got up to inspect the window, and found it open a few inches. I closed the window, and as I grasped the catch to lock it shut I heard a sort of cooing sound coming from outside. Then I heard it again, only it was louder.

I peered out through the glass. Perched on a branch of the

tree that stood outside my window, was an owl. Its huge yellow eyes gazed, unblinking, straight at me through the glass, sending a chill down my spine. The owl gave a drawn-out 'hoot,' then flew away in the darkness.

I ran from the window. I threw myself in my chair. Hugging my robe around me, I remembered what MacDuff had once said: "In Cherokee lore, the owl is the symbol for death."

Shivering, I turned down the lamp and crawled in bed. My mind went back to Brooklyn. I'd seen an owl there too, against a yellow moon. When I woke in the morning, I raised the window shade and peered out. There was no owl gazing in at me.

After breakfast at Byron's, MacDuff went to find Billy and Dixon. I strolled through Melrose Park, and saw tents that had not been in the Park the day before. I stopped to read the signs above each tent. The one farthest from me caught my eye first. It said "Women's Suffrage Headquarters."

Chapter 28

The Suffrage tent stood in a vacant lot, a mere patch of grass and black earth, next to the house belonging to Miss Anthony's friend. A group of men and women had gathered in a semi-circle at the front of the tent. Some of the group sat on the lawn, the others stood, shoulder-to-shoulder, behind them. A woman at the center of the group held a flag on a standard. The flag was emblazoned with a single yellow star representing Wyoming, the only U.S. state that had thus far allowed women the vote.

A photographer prepared to take a picture of the group. He straightened and steadied the tripod, and adjusted the camera lens. The group waited, very still, for the sudden bright flash.

Moving closer to the group, I saw Miss Anthony. She was one of those sitting on the ground, the second person in from the left. She sat next to a man in a dress-up straw hat. She looked straight at the camera, that characteristic little smile playing on her lips.

I saw another interesting face in the group. A man's face, a familiar face, standing in the back row partially hidden behind two other men. MacDuff! I was chagrined. He was looking straight at me when the flash powder exploded.

Miss Anthony was on her feet before the smoke dispersed. The man with the straw hat stood and brushed the seat of his trousers. The woman holding the flag with the yellow star leaned the standard against the tent. MacDuff appeared at my elbow, grinning.

"Hello, Millicent."

"MacDuff! What if that photographer had been the assassin in disguise?"

MacDuff smiled, then stepped around and stood in front of me. "Look over my right shoulder, Millicent, and tell me what you see."

I saw another tent that had not been there before. A banner above it proclaimed, "Family Planning for All!" A display table with stacks of pamphlets on it stood in front of the tent. A large sign next to the pamphlets said: "Free! Take one!" Behind the table stood Mabel Singer.

"I'm going for a stroll, Millicent," MacDuff said.

"And I should go and visit the Family Planning tent."

"I'd go talk to her myself, Millicent, but the lady wouldn't give me the time of day. You know that. Of course, I could go with you."

"If you do, then she won't give me the time of day."

MacDuff shrugged. "Millicent, I think we need to know, first hand, what Mabel really thinks of poor people, especially poor immigrants living in tenement houses."

MacDuff walked away.

Mabel Singer stood behind the display table straightening piles of pamphlets.

"Hello!" I said.

"Oh." She looked up at me, puzzled.

"I'm Millicent Davies. You gave me one of your brochures in Poughkeepsie."

"Oh! Miss Davies, but do forgive me. I cannot possibly remember everyone to whom I give a brochure. There are just too many!"

"But of course, Mrs. Singer."

She smiled and shook my hand.

We exchanged small talk. Soon, I managed to steer our conversation onto immigration. I brought up the plight of the poorer classes of immigrants. During the discussion, Mrs. Singer pointed at a book that lay on the display table face up, a book on Eugenics. She knew I had seen it. I feigned interest. Mrs. Singer picked the book up and handed it to me. I scanned through it quickly.

"Yes," I said, handing it back. "I am familiar with the views of the Eugenics movement."

I did not say that I thought of them as Ku Klux Klan members who cloaked themselves in college degrees instead of bed sheets and pointy hats. Nor did I tell Mrs. Singer that I was a freelance journalist, in newspaper parlance, a muckraker. I did not say that I had once written an article for *The Times* severely criticizing the Eugenics movement. I did not tell her that, honestly, I would rather earn my living by my Remington II serving the literary Muse exclusively as does my idol, Nellie Bly.

"It pays to know one's enemies, Millicent, does it not?" Mrs. Singer said, pointing at the book.

"The Eugenicists are certainly against social programs like yours," I said. "They would view Family Planning for All as but another form of charity for the poor, would they not? And the Eugenicists believe that charity should not be extended to the poor. After all, it would only help keep them alive. Then they would have more and more children, and the charity bill would just grow and grow."

"That's where my organization comes in, Miss Millicent!" Mrs. Singer was now a bundle of excitement.

"Family Planning for All would," she continued, "help these poor people reduce the size of their families, so they might have, perhaps, two or three children, instead of twelve or fourteen, only to have more than half of them die in infancy from diseases bred in those awful tenement houses!" Mrs. Singer paused. "But with fewer children to feed and clothe, poor families could build up their financial resources!"

Mrs. Singer was on her soapbox now, and I was beginning to think I would become her audience of one for the rest of the afternoon.

"Then, Miss Millicent, then they could send one or two of their children to trade school, or perhaps even to college! Why in just one or two generations, the number of people now living in squalor would be greatly reduced. They could live in decent houses where the air was safe to breathe."

I reached over and caught Mrs. Singer by the arm.

"Of course you may perhaps know, Mrs. Singer, that I am an immigrant," I said. "My mother and I came here from England. And we were quite poor."

"From England, oh how very interesting."

My revelation appeared to have taken Mabel Singer by surprise. I was more than a little surprised that she had not seen in my features evidence of my African ancestry.

While we talked, a group of young women gathered at the far end of the table to look at Mrs. Singer's free pamphlets. One of the women picked a pamphlet up, and read from it. Her face turned pink. Another woman stole a peek over the first woman's shoulder. She, too, turned pink, then she raised her hand to her mouth and giggled. Mabel Singer excused herself, then walked over to address the women. Smiling warmly she engaged them in a discussion of her pamphlets.

While Mrs. Singer spoke with the group of women, I glanced inside her tent. The tent flap was open only partway, but I was sure that I saw a man inside. Who was it? I wondered. Her husband? Then another thought struck me. Was the man I saw someone with whom Mrs. Singer was having a clandestine relationship? In any case, I felt compelled to say something.

"Mrs. Singer!" I exclaimed, interrupting her discussion with the young women. I motioned her closer. "Mrs. Singer," I whispered, "there is a man inside your tent. Oh, of course, it must be your husband," I added.

Mrs. Singer went to the tent opening, and looked in. She threw the flap all the way open and turning around laughed out loud.

"Miss Millicent," she exclaimed. "There is no one there."

I looked again. Indeed, there was no one inside. There were some boxes filled with birth control pamphlets, but that was all. However, I saw a place at the left-hand corner in the back of the tent where the canvas was raised. It looked as though someone had made a small opening, and had escaped out the back of the tent. I drew Mabel Singer's attention to the opening.

"Why, I made that opening myself, Miss Millicent, in order to allow for better circulation of air."

"I am so glad that I was mistaken," I said. "But Mrs. Singer!" I shook my finger reprovingly. "We sisters must look out for each other, and a woman traveling alone cannot be too careful."

"Oh, Miss Millicent, you are so right. One must be ever so careful."

I turned to leave. Mabel Singer put her hand on my shoulder, and leaned close.

"Oh, Miss Millicent," she whispered. There was a catch in her voice. "We do love each other a great deal. Please, try to understand."

"My dear, we are sisters. Your secret is safe with me." I said.

I walked away wondering what I had just witnessed. Was the person that I had glimpsed inside Mrs. Singer's tent really her lover? Or was it actually her husband? If it was, in fact, her husband James Singer, then another question presented itself. Were they the ones plotting to kill Miss Anthony, as MacDuff and I once suspected?

Further on, I met up with yet another surprise. Down the dusty path, I came upon the Political Equality tent. Standing behind the table was a short, buxom woman wearing pince-nez.

As soon as she saw me, her face lit up.

"Miss Millicent!"

Emma Goldberg ran out from behind the table. Throwing her arms round my waist, she embraced me until I could scarcely breathe. Then she kissed me warmly on both cheeks.

"I am so happy for to see you in this so beautiful little village!"

"I am so glad to see you, too, Miss Goldberg." I said, and I truly was.

"Oh! We must go for to have tea, Miss Millicent!"

Emma looked toward the tent opening.

"Olga!" she shouted.

A pretty girl of sixteen or seventeen came running out.

"Yes?" the girl brushed a lock of shiny black hair from her eyes with her hand, and tucked it under her headscarf.

"You will please to watch table till I return. I, myself, and this lady, we shall go for to have tea."

"Yes, Emma, the table I will watch. Not to worry."

The girl smiled. Emma and I went to Byron's Café.

Byron was behind the counter when we came in. He raised his arm in a sort of salute.

"Hullo, ladies! Hullo!" Byron said. "Welcome to Byron's Café."

Emma Goldberg and I seated ourselves at a table near the door. Byron walked quickly to our table. Facing Emma he gave an exaggerated bow, then shook her hand like a pump handle.

"It's a real pleasure to see you, Miss Goldberg." he said. "A pleasure to see you as well, Miss Millicent."

"Thank you, Byron," I said, surprised that he had remembered my name, and wondering why he and Emma were acquainted.

The waitress had been sitting at the end of the counter smoking a cigarette when we walked in.

"Beatrice!" Byron walked back behind the counter. "Youse have customers." he growled.

"He is capitalist at heart," Emma whispered after Byron went away. "But a print shop in Buffalo he owns. Union print shop, and he to workers pays almost living wage. Besides, he is willing for to print anarchist pamphlets." Miss Goldberg laughed.

Beatrice crushed her cigarette in an ashtray and came to take our order.

"What do you ladies want?" Beatrice said, her tone unfriendly.

"We came for to have tea, Miss Beatrice." Emma's tone was cold.

So, not only did Emma know Byron, the owner, she knew Beatrice the waitress too. Obviously, there was some unpleasant bond between the two women.

We each ordered tea with biscuits and peach jelly. Beatrice took our order and walked to the counter at the back of the café. Emma touched my arm.

"Beatrice, she does not like me. In same shop we both sweat when I first come to America. In Rochester, where I stay with my sister before going to Manhattan. Beatrice denounce me to Mill Boss when to fellow workers I spoke of organizing union. Boss fire me. I was without job for whole month." Emma leaned towards me, put her lips close to my ear. "I spit on Beatrice when I leave mill." Emma giggled.

Beatrice came with our tea and biscuits. When Beatrice poured, she deliberately tried to spill hot tea on Emma's hand. Emma moved her hand away just in time. Snatching a hatpin from her sleeve, she stabbed the pin into Beatrice's forearm, then yanked the pin back out. Beatrice's face turned red with pain and anger, but she did not yell out. She quickly pressed her apron against the wound to stop the bleeding.

"You dirty Jewess!" Beatrice hissed.

"Would you please for to bring us fresh cream for our tea?" Emma said, without raising her voice.

Beatrice ran behind the counter, then through a door that led to the backroom. She came out a moment later, hat askew, holding a napkin over the hatpin wound.

"I am suddenly feeling ill, Byron!" Beatrice announced in a loud voice. "I must go home!"

Beatrice ran out banging the café door. Byron glanced at us. He shrugged his big shoulders.

After Beatrice left, we both sat quietly sipping our tea and nibbling our biscuits. Suddenly, Emma said, "Oh, Millicent! You remember when last in New York City we spoke, my Sasha and I say Daniello was on way to Europe on steamship?"

"Yes. MacDuff and I interviewed others who verified what you and Sasha told us."

"Well, Miss Millicent." Emma leaned closer and lowered her voice. "I arrive Lily Dale yesterday from Rochester by afternoon train. At Buffalo station I see from coach window a man get on train. This man, he was not tall. His shoulders, they were narrow. His hair, and eyes, they were black, his hair wavy. He had on black hat with wide brim. Miss Millicent! He look like --"

"Tony Daniello," I interrupted.

"Yes!" Emma paused. "But this man had beard, Millicent, thick black beard."

"A black beard?" I smiled.

Emma laughed. "Beard was fake. So maybe stories about Daniello on way to Europe, were fake like beard?"

"It is possible, Emma. Indeed, the stories may be untrue. Did you see this man after you got off the train at the Lily Dale depot?"

"Yes! I did see this same man to get off train. He went with grip on wagon, and go with others across bridge. I am on wagon behind, and I watch."

"Then he must have come through the gate and would now be somewhere in the village!" I felt both excited and uneasy.

"Yes, my sister. I see this man go inside gate. But I not see him again. Not yesterday, not today."

"Emma, my friend, thank you!"

I leaned over and kissed the little anarchist on the cheek. She laughed at my exuberance.

"Now I must go and find MacDuff."

Chapter 29

I found MacDuff rocking in a wicker chair on the Grand Hotel porch and talking with Billy Bergin. When I related Miss Goldberg's story, MacDuff sent Billy to tell Dixon to watch for a bearded man who would, without the beard, resemble Tony Daniello.

"Millicent, according to the hotel clerk there's a thousand people in this little burg already today. It's been a steady stream from the depot to the grounds all day long. The village crews are setting up big tents in the camp grounds."

"Then we had better start looking for our bearded Daniello right now. We know what he looks like, beard or no beard. But one more thing, MacDuff, and this is important! You remember when you sent me to Mrs. Singer's Family Planning table?"

"Of course."

"While I was there, I chanced to glance inside the tent over Mrs. Singer's shoulder. The tent flap was pulled a little to one side, and when I looked in I saw a man."

MacDuff did not seem to hear what I said.

"Just about every house in the village has rooms to let, Millicent."

"I know, MacDuff. But!"

I had just related what I thought was an important piece of information, and MacDuff treated it as though it were last week's news. Why? I wondered.

"We have a lot of rooms and grounds to search. So let's go," MacDuff said. "Here's our story, Millicent. We're reporters, of course, from the *Pittsburg Daily Press*, and we're here to interview speakers for the Political Equality Club. We'll tell the boarding house proprietors we've already interviewed Miss Goldberg, and now want to interview another Political Equality Club speaker. We think the speaker arrived today, from New York City. We'll describe him but claim we don't know his name. We'll try to persuade the proprietor to name somebody, anybody, on her guest list who matches the description Miss Goldberg gave you. If we don't find him at the boarding houses, then we will search the campgrounds and, finally, the hotel. We'll check out Byron's Café, too. And the bathhouse and the Bunch Club. We'll look everywhere there is to look."

It was nearly dark when MacDuff and I finished our investigation. We ended up back at the hotel, tired and discouraged. We stopped at the desk to inquire from the clerk whether anyone looking like the man Emma described had checked in at the Grand.

"Not as far as I know," the clerk said.

At the hotel MacDuff insisted on doing what he called a walk-around, but what I called a waste-of-time.

We checked the parlor first. There was no one in the parlor. We went out onto the first floor porch. Many people were there rocking and conversing, but none of the men resembled the man Miss Goldberg described. There were no sleeping rooms on the first floor, and the hotel dining room had already closed for the night. We climbed the stairs. There was nothing on the second floor porch except empty wicker rocking chairs, and moonlight. The third floor porch was like the second.

Leaving the third floor porch, we went inside and walked down the hall toward our rooms. Halfway down the hall, MacDuff froze.

Chapter 30

MacDuff crouched low to the floor. He cocked his head to the side and listened. His eyes were narrow slits. The image MacDuff presented was so wolf-like it sent a chill down my spine.

MacDuff had heard something. Now I heard it too. MacDuff grabbed my arm. He pressed two fingers to my lips.

Clack clack…clack…clackclackclack…then -- ding! Someone in one of the third floor rooms was typing!

We crept along the carpeted hall past one door, then two doors, then three. Again, MacDuff froze. We now stood outside room three forty-three. The sound came from there. A bar of light shone under the door. MacDuff stepped quickly to the right of the door, his back flat against the wall, his gun in his hand. I stood against the wall to the left of the door.

The sound of the typing machine continued, clackclackclack, ding! Clackclack…

MacDuff rapped on the door with the gun barrel. The clackclackclack of the machine stopped. Chair legs scraped against the wooden floor on the other side of the door, followed by the shuffling of feet. Then the typing resumed. Clackclackclack… Then silence.

MacDuff swung away from the wall. He stood with the revolver pointed at the center of the door, chest high. With his free hand, he grabbed hold of the knob. He turned the knob, and pushed. The door was locked.

"You in there, open up!" MacDuff yelled, stepping to the side.

No response. Nothing, no sound at all now, coming from room three forty-three. I opened my jacket and removed my Iver Johnson.

MacDuff raised his right leg, extended his arms to the sides to balance himself. Then he gave the door a tremendous kick. The lock gave; the door burst open, rebounding slowly after crashing against the wall. Supported by one hinge, the door looked like a drunk trying to stand on one foot. Holding the .38 now in both hands, MacDuff dropped to one knee, and pointed the gun at the center of the room. There was no one there. MacDuff motioned me to stay put. He stood up and lunged into the room.

Unable to stand the suspense, I crept into the room behind MacDuff. Crossing the threshold, my left shoe found a squeaky floorboard. MacDuff who was by then standing about center of the room with his back to me, spun around in a blur and I found myself looking down the barrel of his revolver!

"Damn!" MacDuff hissed, and spun back around.

I moved farther into the room, my heart pounding.

A wall lamp blazed next to the bed. The flame wobbled inside the globe, casting eerie shadows on the walls. Over MacDuff's shoulder, I saw an open window. The blind was up, the curtains swished from side to side.

MacDuff dove at the window. Cautiously, he leaned his head and shoulders out, glanced quickly left and right, then ducked back inside.

A wardrobe with no door stood against the left-hand wall. There were a few articles of clothing hanging inside, women's clothing.

I went over to the wardrobe. Inside on a hanger was a smart-looking short jacket and matching skirt that a woman would wear while traveling, on another hanger a high-necked white blouse. A pair of women's large-size high button shoes stood on the floor of the wardrobe. The clothes and shoes looked new.

An oil lamp burned on a table against the front wall, between the wardrobe and the bed. On the table next to the lamp was a typewriting machine. A sheet of paper stuck out of the carriage. MacDuff came away from the window. He crammed his revolver in his belt, grabbed the paper with both hands, and yanked it out of the machine. He held the paper up to the light. I looked over his shoulder.

MacDuff handed the sheet of paper to me. It was blank, but now we knew beyond all doubt the assassin was here in Lily Dale. I retrieved my bag from the hallway where I had dropped it, and shoved the blank paper inside. Obviously, he had taken the message he had been working on with him when he went out the window, leaving a blank sheet in the carriage.

"Of course you noticed?" MacDuff said.

"I'd have to be blind. Same paper. Done on that."

I flicked the typewriter keyboard with my fingernail. MacDuff turned to leave. I touched his arm.

"The clothes in the wardrobe?"

"Yeah, women's garb, Millicent. But look on the dresser."

There was a shaving mug atop the dresser next to the basin, and a straight razor next to the mug.

"C'mon, Millicent," MacDuff said. "Let's go down and have a talk with the night clerk."

The night clerk, whose name was Jason, was cooperative without being helpful. Oh, he was not lying to us, or trying to cover something up. He was simply not a keen observer. According to Jason, the occupant of room three forty-three was a woman. Of that, he told us, there was no question.

"And a most attractive woman, too, I should have to say," Jason said.

When asked to describe her, Jason said: "She is rather taller than an average woman, with raven hair and ebony eyes, and a complexion like fresh milk. She is a slender, buxom young thing wearing dark glasses…"

"If she had on dark glasses, how do you know she had ebony eyes?" I said.

"Well…" Jason's eyes went temporarily blank. "…well, her eyes must have been dark, since her hair was -- so black!"

It was easy to see that Jason was doing the best he could. As my English Grandmother would have said, Jason had been quite smitten with the woman in room three forty-three.

"What name did she use when she registered?" MacDuff said.

"Why, she registered under her own name, of course. I am quite sure of that!" Jason was indignant.

"Let me see that register," MacDuff said.

Jason gave him a sideways look. MacDuff showed Jason his Private Investigator's license. Jason was impressed, but still reluctant.

"For what reason is the lady being investigated, Mr. MacDuff? You're not implying that she is, well, one of those working girls, shall we say?" Jason coughed.

"No."

"Oh, thank heavens," Jason said. "The reputation of the hotel...."

"Look, Jason, just show me the register!"

Jason fussed nervously with his tie.

MacDuff pulled a five-dollar note from his wallet and set it on the desk. Jason stared at the money. Then his arm shot out as though propelled by a screen door spring. Snatching up the money, he stuffed it in his jacket pocket, and hauled the register from under the desk. He slammed the register down on the desktop, and with a flourish opened it to the current page. Jason gave the register a shove with the heel of his hand. It skidded across the desktop and came to rest at MacDuff's elbow. Then Jason spun around and dashed through a door behind the desk.

"I must go and see about the linens," he said over his shoulder.

MacDuff ran his finger down the guest list, stopping at room three forty-three.

"Miss Abigail Deary," he said. "Newark, New Jersey."

I looked over MacDuff's shoulder. The note next to the name said: "pre-registered by mail, August, ten."

I looked at the register again. "She, that is he, signed the register yesterday at three o'clock, MacDuff."

Jason the night clerk returned from 'seeing to the linens.'

"Well?" Jason said.

MacDuff closed the register and pushed it toward Jason, who put it back under the desk.

"Jason, the person who calls herself 'Miss Abigail Deary' is no longer in room three forty-three," MacDuff said.

"I didn't see her leave," Jason said, looking perplexed.

"The person who occupied room three forty-three crawled out the window onto the 3rd floor porch, ran to the door at the rear of the porch, and slipped inside the hallway. The person walked down the back stairs to the second floor, then down the stairs to the lobby, and out the front door."

"Impossible!" Jason said. He squared his shoulders. "I'd have seen her."

"Jason, during the past hour did you see anyone come down the stairs to the lobby -- anyone at all?" I said. "That is, aside from MacDuff and me."

Jason's brow furrowed. He scratched his chin.

"Yes, I did see someone. A young man came down the stairs, rather hurriedly, as I recall. I spoke as he passed but he did not seem to hear. He passed through the lobby and out the door. I heard him go down the porch steps."

"What did he look like?" MacDuff said.

"Medium height, no, a little taller I think."

"How was he built?"

"Quite slender, I should say. Yes, and narrow at the shoulder."

"What color was his hair?"

"Light brown. No. His hair, you say. It might have been auburn…"

"And his eyes?"

"Well, I do not know the color of the young man's eyes. It is our custom, you see, to lower our gaslights during the late evening hours. The gas was down too low for me to see the color of his eyes as he passed the desk. Actually, it wouldn't have mattered. Even if the gas had been turned up I would not have been able to see the color of his eyes, because he was wearing a hat and the hat was pulled down over his eyes when he passed the desk."

"But you're sure it was definitely a man?"

"Oh, yes. Without a doubt."

Jason 'allowed' as he had better go up and check on room three forty-three. We followed him up the stairs and went inside the room with him.

"Oh my," he said, surveying the damaged door. "What on earth happened here?"

He looked at MacDuff. MacDuff shrugged.

Jason looked around and quickly concluded that Miss

Abigail Deary had indeed checked out, albeit unofficially.

"I wonder how she managed to slip past me? And why on earth didn't she take all of her things?"

MacDuff and I looked at each other. MacDuff rolled his eyes.

"It appears that she was in a hurry to leave," I said. My sarcasm escaped Jason's notice.

"You say you are detectives, Mr. MacDuff. Well, just what is it that you are investigating, and what does it have to do with Miss Deary? I don't think you told me."

"It's a missing wife case, Jason," MacDuff lied. "That's all I can say."

"Oh, I see!" Jason whispered.

We all left the room. Jason tried to close the door, which thanks to MacDuff, was now hanging by one hinge.

"I must find the hotel repairman," Jason muttered.

Jason hurried back down to the lobby. MacDuff and I went to my room to confer.

"I wonder who it was, made up to look like a woman?" I said.

"And to think he carted that machine with him all the way from New York City. Say, MacDuff. Was it a man masquerading as a woman?"

MacDuff grinned. "Or was it the other way around?"

"Wait a minute, Millicent," MacDuff said.

He left the room. He returned a few minutes later carrying the typewriter that had been in room three-forty-three.

"MacDuff!"

"Evidence, Millicent," he said. "I am well within my rights as a private investigator to take it."

We continued our debate over the gender of the person who had rented room three-forty-three.

"It could have been a woman after all," I said, half-joking. "In fact, the shaving mug and straight razor might have been props -- just part of the charade."

"Did you look in the wash basin, Millicent?"

"Well, no."

"There was black stubble floating in it."

"Then the room was not occupied by a woman posing as a man."

"Well, Millicent, whoever it was, it damn sure wasn't Daniello."

A bell went off inside my head. I looked at MacDuff.

"Of course it wasn't Daniello."

MacDuff grinned.

"It couldn't have been."

"Yeah, Millicent. According to those we interviewed, Daniello couldn't use a typewriter if his life depended on it."

We were tired, and knew we had a most stressful day to face in the morning.

MacDuff said goodnight, and headed out the door. The door closed, then opened again.

"Lock it, Millicent, and throw the bolt."

The night was close but I dared not leave my window open. Twice, I woke from a dream, and in the semi-dark I rose to splash my face with water from the basin. I dreamed of opening night at the People's Theater on the Bowery, where I played my first Shakespearian role. I could almost feel the heat from the footlights. I had played one of the witches from Macbeth, and after I went back to sleep lines from the play kept running through my mind.

There was a knock on the communicating door. I woke with a start, and saw MacDuff standing just inside my room.

"Millicent, wake up! We have to go and have breakfast."

"All right!" I said. "Go away now, and close that door! I'll be ready in fifteen minutes."

MacDuff pulled the door shut with a bang.

"I'll meet you on the porch!" he said from his side of the door.

We were both in a wonderful mood. Thank god, I said to myself, that I don't wear one of those stupid corsets. Women who wear them say that it takes half an hour, with help, to lace up one of those straightjackets.

When I stepped out of the lobby, I saw Mac Duff sitting on the porch with some other early risers, all of them smoking and rocking, and watching the mist on the lake rise in the early morning sun. The air was still and humid. It promised to be a sweltering day.

I walked over to MacDuff and touched him gently on the shoulder.

"Morning, Millicent," he said not looking up. "Feeling better now?"

"I'm sorry, MacDuff. You woke me in the middle of a murder."

"I know. You muttered some lines from Macbeth."

"Oh, it makes me shiver to recall! It was the part where Macbeth murders Duncan. Macbeth had just told Lady Macbeth that he had done the deed. He asks if she had heard anything, and Lady Macbeth said, yes, she had heard the owl scream."

"That's the line I heard you say, MacDuff said. 'Yes, I heard the owl scream.'"

"MacDuff."

"Uh huh."

"Just before you heard me say that line, I actually heard --"

"I know, I heard it too."

"That owl screeched, MacDuff, and it was loud!"

"C'mon, Millicent. Let's go eat."

"MacDuff, does it mean..."

"That Miss Anthony is going to die today? Millicent, maybe all it means, is the owl missed its breakfast. Now let's go to Byron's joint."

Chapter 31

"MacDuff, you said yourself that the assassin would think Lily Dale the ideal place to kill Miss Anthony. There will be more than three thousand people in the auditorium today. If the assassin is the fanatical maniac his letters seem to show him to be, he could simply stand up in the audience, gun in hand, and kill Miss Anthony while she stood at the lectern. And how could we stop him? Oh, MacDuff, suddenly it all seems so hopeless."

After a hurried breakfast at Byron's, we went searching for our two agents at large, to review with them our plans for today. But just as we opened the door to leave the café, Billy Bergin showed up. The three of us sat at a table outside and talked.

"You weren't at the hotel, so I knew you'd be here," Billy said.

"How goes the stakeout?" MacDuff said.

"Nothing interesting to report," Billy said.

MacDuff and I told Billy of our adventure of the night before at the Grand Hotel. We told him about the night clerk's description of the man, or woman as the case may be, whom we had surprised at the typing machine.

"Okay," Billy said, "let me get this straight, I mean once and for all. We should all be on the lookout today for a guy in the auditorium who looks like the guy the clerk described to you and Millicent last night…"

Billy's words trailed off.

"Or should we be looking for him dressed up like a woman?"

Billy mopped imaginary sweat from his brow.

"It's a gent we'll all be looking for, Billy, not a woman. When Millicent and I surprised him the guy took a dive out the window. He left his lady's duds in the room."

"He'll stand about five-eight, slender, narrow at the shoulder," I said.

"How will he be dressed?" Billy asked.

"Look around," I said.

Billy looked around. He looked at the men walking by in the street. He looked at himself, then at MacDuff.

"I see what you mean," Billy laughed. "I'll go muddle Dixon's head too."

"Okay," MacDuff said. "And, Billy, I want you and Dixon to meet me and Millicent near the Pagoda at one o'clock."

"That funny little building in Melrose Park by the auditorium?"

"That's the one."

Billy left. MacDuff and I went back to the hotel to prepare for our day, agreeing to meet, properly attired, on the first floor porch.

MacDuff was there when I stepped out of the lobby. At first, I didn't know him. He had slicked down his hair with tonic, and now sported a small mustache with twisted ends. Pinned to the pocket of his green and white striped dress shirt was a small white card that said PRESS. MacDuff looked fine.

I do not think he recognized me at first, either. I had on a businesswoman's jacket that was, I thought, rather too large, over a white blouse with high collar. My hair was shot with gray and pulled back severely in a tight bun at the nape of my neck. I, too, had PRESS pinned to my jacket.

We left the porch and stood among the crowd on Cleveland Drive. I looked up through the canopy of leaves high above my head. There was not a cloud in the sky. Strolling along the street, my arm through MacDuff's, I was amazed at the number of people, and I could hear more trains arriving in the distance, at the depot across the bridge.

Every man and woman I saw, even the children, wore yellow badges prominently displayed to show their support for Women's Suffrage. Everywhere I looked, I saw big yellow ribbons hanging over cottage doors, and flying from porches and awnings. Wide yellow banners stretched from one house to another across all the streets of Lily Dale.

Hundreds of people walked about, most of them dressed in the latest finery. Naturally, there were far more women than men in the crowds along the streets and pathways, far more parasols than bowler hats. Still, there were many more men in Lily Dale than I had seen any other place on Miss Anthony's schedule.

MacDuff and I met Billy and Dixon at the Pagoda, and went over our plans together one last time. We shook hands and wished each other luck.

MacDuff and I showed our Press badges to the person in charge at the door, a Mrs. Pettingel. She handed us each a program, and we were among the first half dozen people to enter the auditorium. MacDuff and I went to our respective positions on the raised platforms.

People streamed in by twos and threes at first, then by the score. A rushing river of bustles, long skirts, and high button shoes, of black frockcoats, bowler hats and walking sticks, flowed through the auditorium main door until all seats were taken. A battalion of ushers then formed a human shield, blocking the entrance. Excited voices filled the auditorium. The auditorium stage was festooned with an all-yellow theme. Yellow flowers, yellow standards, yellow crepe.

Pressing my elbow against my side, I felt my Iver Johnson snug in its holster under my jacket. I saw MacDuff on the platform across the room. He reached a hand inside his coat to check his revolver.

As the crowd quieted down, four women filed onto the stage from behind the blue curtain, stage right. One of the four was very old. According to the program, she was, in fact, more than eighty. She had been Miss Anthony's schoolteacher, a Quaker woman who had the further distinction of being the oldest Suffragist then living. With great care, Miss Anthony helped her former teacher to her chair. It thrilled me to tears.

Two other women came onto the platform and sat down. Then a well-dressed man, tall and official looking, walked from behind the blue curtain and stood behind the lectern, Chairman of the proceedings, Mr. Harrison Barrett. Mr. Barrett welcomed the women seated on the platform, and welcomed the three thousand of us sitting or standing in the crowded auditorium. As much as humanly possible, MacDuff and I watched everyone.

The auditorium sidewalls were fitted with large wooden shutters. These shutters had been removed, so that another thousand people could watch and listen from outside the auditorium.

MacDuff and I knew that Billy and Dixon were outside too; doing their best to watch those for whom there was no room inside the auditorium.

A woman from the nearby city of Jamestown, NY, Kate O. Peate, rose and said some opening words. Then a chorus of singers marched out on the platform and stood behind the speaker's chairs. Two men wheeled a grand piano onto the stage.

Professor Carlton Weber walked across the stage and sat down at the piano. Professor Weber then accompanied the chorus in a rendition of the song "Wyoming," to honor Miss Anthony and to acknowledge the state of Wyoming as the first to allow women freedom to vote. It brought tears to people's eyes. During the applause, a woman seated nearby said to her friend:

"Professor Weber is a truly great accompanist, and is himself a wonderful singer and pianist. I have heard him perform many times."

Now Chairman Barrett introduced Miss Anthony. Her words were simple and straight forward, her voice soft but confident.

While Miss Anthony spoke, I studied the faces of the people. They were entranced. Miss Anthony had made each of the three thousand people in the auditorium feel as though she had spoken directly, and especially, to them.

"My friends." Miss Anthony began to gather up her notes.

"My friends, I have heard many of you here refer to this unusual village of like-minded souls as a religious community. It is that, indeed, and I am proud beyond words that you have invited me to share my thoughts with you today." Miss Anthony cleared her throat.

"But it was reported recently in the Press that I am a godless woman, because I do not get down on my knees and pray. But the God of my understanding does not require that of me. Yet I do pray. Indeed, as a dedicated suffragist and worker for equal rights, every day of my life I pray with my work!"

"Therefore, my friends, I invite you all to go forth and pray with me today."

The auditorium exploded in thunderous sustained applause.

As the applause died, Miss Anthony walked away from the podium. When she disappeared behind the curtain and was, I thought, on her way to the stage door, a man standing across the auditorium just inside the main entrance doors caught my attention. I removed my opera glasses from my bag, and focused them on the man's face. I did not like what I saw. On the faces of everyone else in the auditorium, I saw admiration and, indeed, adoration. On the face of the man standing near the entrance doors, magnified six times by the glasses, I saw a look of hatred such as I had never seen on anyone's face before.

Otherwise, he looked like most other men in the auditorium, who were now gathering up their hats and programs preparing to leave. The man was of medium height with dark hair and handlebar mustaches. He had on black pants and jacket, and a bowler hat. When he turned and glanced briefly in my direction, I saw his face straight on. I did not think he was the man the clerk at the Grand Hotel described to us the night before. Possibly, I thought, he looked a little like the man Emma Goldberg saw, sans the fake black beard. Well, I thought, maybe Daniello and the assassin just happen to look alike. As I continued studying his features, the man darted out the door. I saw MacDuff run out into the Park after him. Then, I lost sight of them both. They had disappeared in the gathering crowd outside in the Park.

Yelling "PRESS! PRESS! Let me through!" I inched my way through the crowd to an exit door. Then I struggled through the crowd outside, at the back of the auditorium, and pushed, and shoved, until I reached the front of the building. By then the crowd inside the auditorium had all gone out, so now Melrose Park was as crowded as the auditorium had been.

Miss Anthony, meanwhile, was nowhere to be seen. I thought she must have gone out the stage door. If so, I hoped she had returned safely to the home of her friend in Melrose Park. My heart beat wildly as I pushed through the crowd, trying to find MacDuff.

Finally, I found him. He was sitting on a bench near the Lassing-Tilton house, talking with Billy Bergin. I plopped breathlessly down between them. To an on-looker, we were three excited Lily Dale tourists.

"I saw you follow a man out of the auditorium, then I lost sight of you in the crowd," I said to MacDuff.

"And then I lost sight of the man, Millicent."

"Too damn many people," Billy said. "Reminds me of the Hester Street Market on Friday afternoon, about an hour before the start of Jewish Sabbath."

I described the man I had seen through my glasses. MacDuff said my description matched the man that he had seen. Billy said he thought that he and Dixon had seen the same man, when they were watching for Miss Anthony to come out the stage door. The man was among a group of perhaps thirty people walking along that end of the auditorium. Billy said he was certain that Miss Anthony had come out the stage door with Chairman Barrett, and the two of them headed toward the Lassing-Tilton house. According to Billy, Dixon ran ahead and arrived at the house first. He went up on the porch and peeked in the windows, and saw no one there who shouldn't have been.

"You're sure she's still in the house, Billy?"

"Yes," he said. "She's still there. Barrett stayed maybe five minutes, then he came out and walked back towards the auditorium."

"And, MacDuff, Dixon said the lady who owns the house?"

"Mrs. Lassing-Tilton. Yeah, Billy?"

"Well, Dixon says she never did leave the house. I mean she was there the whole time. When Miss Anthony got there with Mr. Barrett, and knocked on the door, the Lassing-Tilton dame had to unlock the door and let them in."

"So they are both there now, Miss Anthony and her friend Mrs. Lassing-Tilton," I said. I wondered why Miss Anthony's friend hadn't gone to hear her speak, but glad she hadn't because it meant that no one was likely to have gone inside the Lassing Tilton residence to wait for Miss Anthony.

"Better go and check again with Dixon, Billy," MacDuff said. "Millicent and I will wait here for your report."

Billy made his way along the path through the crowd, returning a few minutes later. Billy said he was certain Miss Anthony was in the house, as was Mrs. Lassing-Tilton. Dixon told Billy that nobody else went in or out of the house since he, Dixon, had been watching the place. Neither agent saw any suspicious person anywhere near the house.

"Okay, Billy," MacDuff said. "Make sure Dixon stays put. For now, you should continue watching the front door from here in the park."

Chapter 32

MacDuff took hold of my hand. He stood, pulling me up with him.

"C'mon, Millicent," he said. "We're going to have a talk with Susan B. Anthony."

"MacDuff, she'll think we're from the Press. She won't even answer the door! She doesn't even like women reporters, and she absolutely loathes those of your gender. You know that, MacDuff! We are still using that cover, I assume. Newspaper reporters?"

"Uh huh," MacDuff said, pulling me towards the house. "It's time to tell Miss Anthony what's going on. And get her to cooperate. Her life depends on it, and so might ours."

"But you know how obstinate she can be!"

"Look, Millicent. You know Miss Anthony once granted Nellie Bly an interview, right? You've been quoting from Nellie's piece ever since we left Manhattan."

"Yes, but… "

"No buts. We're going to try. We have to. Now, let's go." MacDuff tugged on my arm. Then he said, "Look, Millicent. I know I can rely on you to break down Miss Anthony's resistance, after I break down the Lassing-Tilton lady's front door."

"MacDuff! You wouldn't!"

He stared at me from out of that blue eye.

Oh, oh, I said to myself. I thought back to Brooklyn. That was not the first time MacDuff had made kindling wood out of someone's door.

MacDuff and I strode from our bench to Miss Anthony's temporary residence. We stopped and stood in front of the house, where the sidewalk met the porch steps. MacDuff put his hand on my shoulder. He looked at me narrowly.

"Forget the newspaper reporter cover," MacDuff said. "Here's where we drop all disguises and pretense, Millicent. I'm MacDuff, Private Investigator. You're Millicent Davies, my partner. No more play acting."

MacDuff and I climbed the steps onto the porch, side-by-side. MacDuff knocked on the door. We both took a respectful step back, and waited. The door opened two or three inches. A gray eye belonging to Mrs. Lassing-Tilton peered out. A grayish-yellow strand of hair hung down between the door and the doorjamb.

"It's important that we speak to Miss Anthony," MacDuff said to the gray eye. "We know she's here."

"Reporters?"

It was not a friendly voice.

"My name is MacDuff. I'm a private investigator. This is my partner, Miss Millicent Davies."

"Miss Anthony is resting, and must not be disturbed," the woman said.

MacDuff stepped aside. It was my turn to address the gray eye.

"Whom do I have the pleasure of addressing, madam, Mrs. Lassing-Tilton, I presume?"

She did not answer. I stepped closer to the door.

"We are not reporters," I said. "We are as we have said, private investigators. We are here at the request of our client who happens to be a close friend of Miss Anthony. We are here because Miss Anthony's life is in great danger.

Abruptly, the door closed. A bolt slammed shut. A moment later, the door opened again, a little wider this time.

"Miss Anthony has instructed me to tell you she has no need of your services."

Once more, the woman closed the door. Once more, the bolt slammed shut. Through the front window, to the right of the door, I caught a glimpse of a slender figure in black move quickly across the room, then disappear in the shadows.

"It was her, MacDuff. That was Miss Anthony!"

MacDuff took a deep breath. His coat stretched tight across his chest, his neck muscles bulged. He clenched his jaws, made a fist, and pounded on the door.

"Miss Anthony!" MacDuff yelled.

People walking past looked at us. MacDuff shot them his

blue-eyed gaze. They hurried away. MacDuff took three steps back, and stared at the varnished oak door. He drew his lips away from his teeth.

"Oh no," I thought. "He is going to do it, he is going to break down the door, and the police are going to come, and…"

I shall never know whether MacDuff actually would have broken down that door, because the door opened once again. This time the door swung wide, and there she stood, the great lady herself, Miss Susan B. Anthony.

"Well?" Her tone was not unfriendly, but Miss Anthony did not step aside to let us in.

MacDuff showed his private license.

She gave it a glance.

"So, Mr. MacDuff and Miss Millicent, the two of you believe, erroneously I am sure, that someone wants to kill me today. You are both private detectives, though certainly not Pinkerton agents, as I happen to know Pinkerton would never hire you my dear, a woman. In any case, you are detectives. Now who, may I ask, did hire you?"

MacDuff nodded to me.

"Miss Anthony," I said. "We were hired by your friend Mrs. Isabella Beecher Hooker."

Miss Anthony threw back her head and laughed.

"Of course! Of course!" she said. "Who but Belle, dear Belle. And who, or what, I wonder, put the bee in Belle's bonnet? The whole thing is ridiculous."

I looked at MacDuff.

"We have proof. Show her, Millicent."

I removed the letters from my bag and handed them to Miss Anthony.

"They are arranged in the order received." I said.

Miss Anthony looked at the first letter, the one which had been addressed to Belle and which Belle had given to us when she came to our consulting rooms.

"Belle showed this one to me the day she received it," Miss Anthony said with a shrug.

"Miss Millicent and Mr. MacDuff, more than once in the past someone has threatened to harm me. In Rochester, NY, for example, many, many years ago, I made a speech in a park on behalf of Woman's Suffrage. A man in the crowd took offense, that is, he did not agree with my ideas. He threatened to horsewhip me, and then hang me by the neck from one of the trees in the park."

"We know the story, Miss Anthony," MacDuff interrupted. "You gave the speech anyway, and nothing came of the threat."

"Miss Anthony," I began again. "The person who wrote those letters followed you here." I reached out and touched Miss Anthony's hand. "He followed you all the way from New York City. He is an assassin. We do not know exactly who he is, or whom he represents other than himself. But, Miss Anthony, we do know this: he intends to kill you. Please, you must believe us!"

Miss Anthony looked at me, then at MacDuff, then at the clock on the mantel. She handed the letters back to me.

"It will soon be time for my evening repast," she said. "Then I must prepare to go by coach to the Fredonia Opera House. It is their Grand Opening. I must be ready to leave Lily Dale soon. So if you will both excuse me?"

"Okay, Millicent," MacDuff said. "Let's go."

As we turned to leave Miss Anthony addressed us both:

"I am sorry for any inconvenience I may have caused you. However, I do feel that my friend Belle is spending a great deal of her husband's money to protect me from what I am certain shall prove to have been a bothersome, though expensive practical joke after all."

MacDuff turned and faced Miss Anthony, then looked at me. Anticipating his plan, I nodded.

"Miss Anthony, will you allow Miss Millicent, my partner, to go with you this evening?"

"Yes, Miss Anthony, may I please have that honor?"

"Oh, dear me. I'm afraid I cannot allow that. My friend Mrs. Cornelia Lassing-Tilton shall be with me. Our box seats have already been reserved."

"Perhaps I could occupy a third chair in the box?"

"Oh, no, Miss Millicent. My friend Cornelia assures me that there isn't room for a third party. Besides, my dear, I have never before required protection when attending the opera, not a woman's protection, or a man's. Nor do I need protection on this occasion, thank you all the same." Her voice was firm, but not arrogant.

Before we left, MacDuff looked at Miss Anthony. "One more thing, Miss Anthony. All of us, Millicent and I, and our two agents, have sworn never to tell the official police or the press, or anyone else for that matter, about the plot to kill you. You still have our word on that, no matter what."

Miss Anthony reached out and put her hand on MacDuff's shoulder, her other hand on mine.

"I believe you," she said. I want you both to know that."

Miss Anthony turned around and went back inside. The door closed, the dead bolt shot home.

MacDuff and I walked to Byron's to have dinner and to confer.

"Of course we shall be going to the opera this evening, MacDuff."

"That's where the assassin will be, Millicent. It's been on my mind since..."

"Since we got the letter at the Buffalo station, with the reference to 'high opera!' It's been on my mind too."

"Millicent, what I'd like to know is how the assassin knew when he wrote that letter, that Miss Anthony and her friend Cornelia would go to the opera tonight?"

Before our order came, Billy Bergin showed up. He had followed us, leaving Dixon to watch the Lasing-Tilton residence. So the three of us sat and planned our evening at the Fredonia Opera House. We needed a coach for the evening. That was the first order of business, and Byron was able to help us.

"We don't need a driver, Byron, just a coach. Millicent and I and our friends want to go to the new opera house in Fredonia, which we understand is having its grand opening this evening."

"Why don't youse take the train? It's a lot less money," Byron said.

"We don't want to take the train, Byron," MacDuff growled.

"Well, Lily Dale rents out coaches," Byron said. "If youse got money to burn, go see Andy Waters, at number Eighteen First Street. He's in charge of the carriage rentals. Andy will take youse up to the barns."

Andy, who had bright red hair and a big friendly smile, walked with us to the barns at the end of South Street. Leaving his house, I could not help noticing the beautiful flowers next door. I saw cosmos, hollyhocks, roses, morning glories, asters, daisies, snapdragons, and phlox. Tall sunflowers, the official flower of the religion of Spiritualism, all in a row in back, were just coming into bloom. It was the most beautiful border garden I had seen since leaving England. A woman, who appeared to be in her early seventies, danced among the myriad blossoms like an elderly Sprite.

A shiny black coach hitched to a handsome pair stood in front of one of the barns. A boy stood vigorously applying wax to one of the coach doors.

"We'll take that one, Mr. Waters." MacDuff paid the fee. Andy accepted with a smile and a glad hand. He gave the coach a last minute flick of the rag, patted each horse on the neck, and stuffed the cash in an envelope.

Billy drove to the hotel so MacDuff and I could don appropriate garb for a night at the opera. Then Billy went to Byron's to pick up sandwiches for himself and Dixon. They'd eat them on the way. When we walked out the hotel lobby door, Billy was waiting for us on the porch.

"There's a fancy rig standing at the Lassing-Tilton house waiting for the old ladies to come out," Billy said. "We better be ready to follow it quick. Dixon's waiting for us near the gate."

"Then let's go!" MacDuff said. "Billy, you take the reins."

Billy smiled. He had once worked as a New York City cabbie, his only legitimate job before going to work for us. He drove us in a cloud of dust down Cleveland Drive to South Street, stopping at a place near the Lily Dale entrance gate where we could watch the coach that waited for Miss Anthony and her friend.

Dixon sauntered out of the doorway of the Telegraph Office. He came over to our coach and climbed in.

"There they come out of the house now," Dixon said, pointing.

The driver climbed down from his high perch and helped the women into the coach. The coach rolled out the Lily Dale gate. We followed at a discreet distance. We rumbled across the plank bridge, bounced over the railroad tracks beyond the Iroquois Hotel. We turned right at Glasgow Road and followed the other coach along the well-travelled dirt road that ran from Lily Dale to Fredonia. According to Byron, it was the shortest route.

It was only ten miles to Fredonia, but the road twisted and turned, and went up and down steep hills. Miss Anthony's and her friend's coach moved slowly, and so the trip would take at least an hour. During the journey, we kept watch out the back of the coach to see whether we were being followed. We saw no one.

Chapter 33

Crossing Main Street in Fredonia, we saw Miss Anthony's coach stop in front of the new brick and stone Opera House. Miss Anthony and her friend Cornelia got out and went inside. MacDuff and I got out of our coach half a block from the Opera House entrance. Then Billy and Dixon drove round back to the stables in the alleyway behind the building, where there was a boy to watch the coach and to care for the horses. Our agents would complete a thorough investigation of the Opera House exterior, checking exit doors and windows. Afterwards, before the curtain went up, Billy would meet MacDuff in the Opera House lobby to report his and Dixon's findings.

Their tickets having been paid for in advance, Miss Anthony and Cornelia were ushered directly to their balcony box seats. MacDuff and I went inside and purchased our tickets. We showed our tickets along with our fake *New York Sun* press cards to the volunteer usher, who was lugging several pounds of gemstones around with her. Diamonds and rubies, mostly. We begged the usher to seat us as close as possible to Miss Anthony and Cornelia's private box. At first, the wealthy volunteer refused. I just then happened to mention to the usher, but only as an aside, that our story about the new opera house would be syndicated, and that her name could appear in the article.

After we had secured seats close to Miss Anthony's and Cornelia's private loge, MacDuff went down to the lobby alone to confer with Billy. He returned minutes later and settled himself in the small theater seat.

"Billy says he and Dixon found two rear exits that give on an alley. There's a stage door for the cast, and two big double doors for hauling props in and out. There's one ground floor exit on the right-hand side of the building that opens on an alley, another one that gives on Temple Street. That accounts for all the doors, not including the front main entrance."

"Too many doors, MacDuff, if you ask me."

"But they're all at street level."

"Ah! Then we do not have to watch second-story doors too." I paused. "Except that one."

I pointed at an EXIT sign above a door almost directly across the aisle from us.

"I know," MacDuff said. "We have to talk about that door."

MacDuff and I occupied seats next to the narrow aisle that ran along the right hand wall. We were directly behind the brass railing that curved round the first row of balcony seats. MacDuff was on the aisle, I sat next to him, on his left. The private box occupied by Miss Anthony and her friend was only six or seven feet away, straight ahead of us. The worrisome exit door was directly across the aisle from the back of the private box.

MacDuff looked at his watch. "Half an hour till show time," he said.

Miss Anthony and her friend were hidden from our view by black curtains that covered both sides, as well as the back of the private enclosure. To enter or leave, the occupants need only separate the curtains at the back. One good thing was that MacDuff could easily reach the back of the enclosure or the exit door, in two strides.

As I studied the situation, I saw Miss Anthony's bonneted head lean out from the front of the box, peer over the railing down at the packed house below, and then disappear again behind the curtain. I was certain that it was Miss Anthony, for she had on her signature red silk shawl.

MacDuff was watching me. "You've seen what could happen, Millicent?"

"Yes," I said. "I see only two ways the assassin could get close enough to kill Miss Anthony. He could come up the balcony stairs from the lobby, sneak down the aisle past our seats, then jump inside the private box." I paused, felt my heart skip a beat. "Or he could come out of that EXIT door. But those are the only two ways."

MacDuff saw the look on my face. "Yet, the situation is in our favor, Millicent, not the assassin's. We're in the best possible spot to stop him. Unless we both fall asleep, nobody could come down our side of the aisle, or in from that EXIT door without one of us seeing him."

I nodded assent, but I was not convinced. "What if there's more than one assassin, MacDuff?"

"There are still only those same two ways to get at Miss Anthony. And they'd still have to get past us." MacDuff gave his shoulder holster a pat through his coat.

While watching for trouble, I allowed myself a cursory glance at the décor of the new Opera House, and took a quick look at the several hundred people who were there for the opening performance.

Of course, the Fredonia Opera House was no Carnegie Hall, which opened in Manhattan the past April with a program by Peter Tchaikovsky. Yet, the new Fredonia House had a certain charm. Adorned with a great many gaslights, a grand chandelier hung from the ceiling at the center of the House. A single valve controlled the dozens of small gaslights circling the fixture. Therefore when the performance began, all of the chandelier globes would go dark at once.

Leaning forward, I peered at the people seated on the main floor. Even in the dim houselights, I could easily tell the men from the women. I need only pay attention to hats and to notice the difference between bowlers and birds. Many women wore diamonds and other precious gems. They sparkled in the gas light.

Naturally the men wore the usual Victorian uniform, which was the same in Fredonia as in New York City. Black trousers, black hat, black vest, black swallowtails, white shirt with detachable collar, everything stiff and starched. Of course, there was the inevitable gold watch on a gold chain tucked inside the vest pocket. I noticed one thing different about the Opera House uniform worn by men in Fredonia. Few of the men carried walking sticks. Looking again at the people round us, I must admit that all of the women as well as the men were more appropriately dressed than we were for a night at the opera.

Having finished my inspection of the House interior and its patrons, I glanced at MacDuff. He was crouched low in his seat, knees drawn up, elbows resting on his knees, fingertips pressed together. He stared intently at the black curtains hiding Miss Anthony and Mrs. Lassing-Tilton from view.

But I knew that MacDuff was watching in his mind a performance that had already begun. In MacDuff's mind, a stage had already been set. Players, poised to speak, waited for cues. Action was about to begin.

Just then the lights dimmed. A tall blond-haired man in tails, the house manager, stepped out of the wings, stage right, and walked to the center of the stage. Raising his arms, he waved white gloved hands above his head. The voices of the people died, slowly. Blond hair and white shirt aglow in the footlights, the tall man raised his voice above the final murmur of the crowd.

"Ladies and gentlemen!" he shouted, "Welcome to the grand opening of the 1891 Fredonia Opera House!"

The audience applauded. The manager cleared his throat. He waved his hands again.

"Opera Lovers, friends, if you have not already done so, please remove your hats, that those behind you might better see the show."

Hats came off with a flutter. The manager took a deep breath.

"And now it is my great pleasure to give you: Ruddigore!"

The manager strode quickly across the stage into the wings. The house lights dimmed, the orchestra pit came alive, and with a great kettledrum roll and crashing of cymbals, the curtain rose.

I was aware only peripherally of the action during the first act. My attention was, of course, otherwise engaged. MacDuff had exited the theater of his mind, and now we both watched the curtained enclosure where Miss Anthony and Cornelia sat watching the play.

Act I finished to a storm of applause, followed by a brief intermission. MacDuff and I held our breath, hoping that neither Miss Anthony nor her friend would leave their seats. They did not.

The house lights dimmed, and then brightened again, signaling that the second act would soon begin. The house lights dimmed once more, and act two, the final act, of Ruddigore began.

As the curtain rose, MacDuff whispered:

"Millicent, my Italian is a little rusty. Ruddigore, what exactly does it mean?"

"Loosely translated, MacDuff, it refers to, well, a bloody mess."

Had I not been entirely focused on watching everyone round us, and watching the exit door across the aisle, like the audience I, too, would have been caught up in the music and drama and madness of Gilbert and Sullivan's play about a family of ghosts.

Suddenly, near the end of the second, and final, act, MacDuff grabbed hold of my wrist and squeezed down hard.

Chapter 34

"Millicent," he breathed in my ear. "Look!"

Slowly, the exit door across the aisle began to open. MacDuff stiffened. Leaning forward, he placed a foot in the aisle. Slowly, noiselessly the door opened more and more. A white glove appeared in the space between the door and the edge of the casing. A sliver of white wrist showed between the glove and a black coat sleeve.

Suddenly, the exit door flew wide open! A man disguised as one of the characters from the play, a Baronet from Ruddigore Castle, charged out of the doorway.

"Now, Millicent!" It was a whispered shout.

MacDuff bounded from his seat.

Parting the curtain with the barrel of his gun, the assassin lunged inside the box occupied by Miss Anthony and her friend Cornelia. MacDuff dove in after him.

There was a great commotion behind the black curtains. A shot rang out! Cornelia, her face a mask of terror, flew out from behind the curtains and ran past me. Immediately, another figure ran out, Miss Anthony. "Thank God!" I said aloud. With surprising speed Miss Anthony fled up the aisle close on Cornelia's heels. Both women ran toward the balcony stairs, then down the stairs to the lobby.

I leaped inside the private box, revolver in hand. Another pistol shot! So close to my face it rendered me temporarily blind and deaf. I felt a sharp burning sensation on my temple, where I had been struck by gunpowder when the gunman's pistol discharged. MacDuff had forced the assailant's gun hand away from my face a bare instant before the gun went off, so that the bullet barely missed. I heard the tinkling of glass when the bullet meant for me struck one of the gas lamps on the grand chandelier.

The gunshot produced a burst of light like the sudden bright flash of a photographer's torch, which illuminated for a split second the struggle taking place as MacDuff and I fought behind the curtains against the man with the gun.

The assailant was devilishly strong. Despite our efforts, he broke away. He leaped over the brass railing. Still brandishing the gun he landed on his feet on top of a piece of scenery, and then jumped from there down onto the stage. Recovering his balance, he ran across the stage into the wings, and disappeared.

MacDuff and I both had our guns trained on the fleeing man, but neither of us dared fire for fear of inadvertently shooting one of the actors or crewmembers who ran frantically around on stage below.

MacDuff and I turned to each other at the same moment, and each saw the other had escaped being shot.

"Where's Miss Anthony, Millicent?" MacDuff shouted.

"Just before I joined you in the fracas, I saw her and Cornelia run up the aisle toward the balcony stairs. Both appeared unhurt!"

MacDuff and I could barely hear each other, for pandemonium had broken out inside the Fredonia Opera House. The aisles were jammed with people screaming and shoving, trying to exit the building. Understandably, no one was trying to reach the Exit door the gunman had used.

"C'mon, Millicent!" MacDuff yelled.

MacDuff and I ran out the back of the loge, across the aisle, then through the same exit door the assailant had come out of only moments ago. To our great fortune, the door was ajar. We dashed down a short corridor, MacDuff in the lead, then down some stairs that led to the double doors at the back of the theater used to bring in props. The doors were open.

"Here's where our man made his grand exit," MacDuff said.

I followed MacDuff out into the alleyway. Just then Billy Bergin came running from the right-hand corner of the building.

"MacDuff!" Billy came rushing up to us. "What happened?"

"The assassin came out these doors. Didn't you see him!"

"Someone in costume came out just before I saw you. He ran past me down the alley, then disappeared around the corner where the stables are!"

Now Dixon came tripping down the alley from the other side of the building, firing questions at us on the run.

"Where's Miss Anthony? Is she still inside, is she okay?"

"Hold on, Dixon! Hold on!" MacDuff shouted.

"MacDuff, watch out!" I yelled.

A man in a two-wheeler raced toward us from the direction of the stables. He careened the carriage close to the building, forcing us to scramble back inside the Opera House through the open double doors. The carriage clattered past on the cobblestones, and the driver raised a fist and shouted, "I'll kill you yet, all of you!"

MacDuff and I ran out in the alley just in time to see the carriage fly around the corner onto Temple Street, and head toward Lily Dale. MacDuff sent Dixon to the front of the Opera House to find Miss Anthony and Cornelia.

"We'll meet you there!" MacDuff shouted as Dixon, running like an Olympian, disappeared round the Temple Street side of the Opera House.

MacDuff and I and Billy ran down the alley to the stables, and piled into our coach. Billy cracked the whip and drove quickly round to the front of the Opera House. When we stopped at the corner of Temple and Park, Dixon appeared at the coach window.

"She's gone!" Dixon yelled. "Miss Anthony and her friend climbed in their coach, and went that way!" Dixon pointed down Temple Street. "An' I saw the assassin go off in the same direction, only he was a couple blocks ahead of the coach that Miss Anthony and her friend was in. But MacDuff, I don't think them women or their driver know that!"

"That means the assassin can just pull off the road someplace," I exclaimed, "wait for them to catch up, and then kill Miss Anthony!"

"Dixon, jump in!" MacDuff yelled. Dixon climbed in, slamming the coach door shut.

"Now go like hell, Billy. We've got to overtake Miss Anthony's coach before it's too late!"

Billy cracked the whip and the horses lunged ahead.

By then Temple Street was filled with coaches and cabs, and people. A policeman stood at the next corner trying to direct traffic. Billy whipped the horses into a gallop, and headed straight

185

at him. Cursing and shouting, the policeman stood in the middle of the street frantically waving his arms. Billy swerved the coach out around just in time, thus avoiding what surely would have been a deadly collision. I felt both right-hand wheels leave the cobblestones, then a sudden jolt when they came back down.

Glancing over my shoulder as we flew through the intersection at Main Street and Temple, I saw the policeman, in the circle of yellow light under the gas lamp, take off his helmet and hurl it at us. It bounced along the street before rolling into the gutter against the curb. I could not help laughing.

I leaned out the side window of the coach and looked down the road ahead. I saw the side lamps of a coach racing away in the distance.

"That must be them!" I shouted to MacDuff who was on the front seat next to Billy.

"Yes! Catch them, Billy!" MacDuff yelled.

Billy caught up to Miss Anthony's coach a few minutes later, and pulled alongside. MacDuff shouted at the driver to stop. Instead, he whipped the horses faster. MacDuff stood up, losing his bowler to the wind. Holding on to the coach seat with one hand, he pointed his gun at the driver.

"I said stop those horses. Now!"

The driver pulled back hard on the reins, and stopped the coach at the side of the road. MacDuff jumped down from our coach, threw open the door of the other coach, and yelled:

"Miss Anthony! Tell your driver what's going on!"

Miss Anthony shouted to the driver: "Melvin, someone is trying to kill me. It is true."

She identified MacDuff and me, and our agents. "They are only trying to stop the assassin," she said. MacDuff asked Melvin whether there was an alternate route back to Lily Dale. He said there was.

"But that route takes a lot longer," Melvin said, "because on that road we'd have to go up a mile-long hill, and it's plenty steep. Why, I'd have to walk the horses most of the way up."

"Is it a well-traveled road?" MacDuff said.

"No, on account'a the hill."

"Good," MacDuff said. "We don't think the man we're after is from around here, so he won't know about that road. He'll wait somewhere along the road we used earlier when we drove from Lily Dale to Fredonia. He'll think there'll be a place along the way where he can stop Miss Anthony's coach. Or he'll try to reach Lily Dale a long time before us, and make an attempt on her life when she gets there."

MacDuff looked at Melvin. "I want you to take the road that goes up the long hill. Dixon will go with you. He's armed."

Dixon pulled his coat aside, showing the butt of his .45 caliber revolver. Melvin grinned.

"Jump in with the ladies, Dixon," MacDuff said.

Dixon joined Miss Anthony and Cornelia.

"See you folks in Lily Dale!" Melvin said.

"One more thing, Melvin," MacDuff said.

"Yes sir?"

"When you arrive, stay with Dixon and the women till Millicent and I show up. There are things we'll all need to talk over before we go home tonight, that is if we're all..."

He stopped abruptly. I know what you were going to say, MacDuff, I said to myself. You mean, "If we're all still alive."

"Yes, sir, Mr. MacDuff," Melvin said. "I'll be sure and wait."

Melvin snapped the reins, and the coach pulled away. We watched it turn at the corner and head for the alternate route. MacDuff and I and Billy followed the assassin, using the other road.

The night was clear, the moon bright. We could easily see in the distance the dust raised by the assassin's carriage. When the carriage dipped down a hill or rounded a curve, and was for a moment out of sight, I wondered whether the assassin had found a good place from which to ambush us. Then with us out of the way, he could pursue his plan to kill Miss Anthony without our further interference. But he would still have Dixon to reckon with.

About two miles from Lily Dale, we saw him silhouetted against the sky at the top of a hill. Five minutes later, we were atop that same hill. I could see Cassadaga Lake in the distance, and on the far shore gaslights twinkling in the windows of the Grand Hotel.

The assassin turned onto the road that went from the depot across the plank bridge to the Lily Dale entrance gate. As we turned onto the same road, MacDuff grabbed Billy's arm.

"Now, Billy, now!" MacDuff shouted.

I braced myself. Billy urged the horses on with the whip. I held on tight as the coach bounced crazily over the railroad tracks and rumbled across the bridge.

We came to a bouncing halt at the gate in front of the ticket booth. A young man peeked out of the little window. His face was white.

"I don't have time to explain!" MacDuff yelled. "Just tell me which way that other coach went after he passed through the gate!"

"W…w…well…" the poor man stuttered.

"Damn it, man! Which way?" MacDuff shouted. "And open that gate now!

"He went to the—the—the—he went that way!"

The gateman pointed to the right. MacDuff jumped out, pushed open the gate, and climbed back in the coach. Billy snapped the whip over the horses' heads, and we lurched through the Lily Dale entrance gate.

"Look!" I shouted, as Billy drove onto the grounds.

There was a carriage flying up South Street hill toward the Lily Dale woods.

"I see him," MacDuff said, talking fast. "Billy, I'll take over the driving now. You stay here by the gate and wait for Miss Anthony's carriage. When they arrive, go with them to the Lassing-Tilton house at Melrose Park. You and Dixon and Melvin stay there and keep Miss Anthony safe, and Billy, be on the lookout in case there's an accomplice."

"You can count on Dixon and me, MacDuff." Billy jumped down from the carriage. MacDuff took the reins and we galloped up South Street hill in pursuit of the assassin. In the light of the street lamp ahead, we saw him cross East Street at the top of the hill and drive toward the stables.

Chapter 35

At the stables, we found the carriage empty, the horse sweating and exhausted, but the assassin nowhere in sight.

"What's that?"

MacDuff heard something, a twig breaking.

"There he goes into the woods, MacDuff!"

We jumped down from our coach, and ran toward the woods. I paused to slip out of my skirt, under which I had on a pair of MacDuff's black trousers. I stuffed my skirt in my shoulder bag, stashed the bag under a bush. I patted my side. My Iver Johnson was snug in its holster under my arm.

We saw the path the assassin used to enter the woods. MacDuff ran in after him. I followed close behind MacDuff. My heart raced, and I felt at that moment a sense of danger such as I have never felt before.

The assassin chose one of the paths MacDuff and I had seen on the map. MacDuff moved down the path in the moonlight, crouched close to the ground. A wolf stalking its prey. My heart leaped. I caught a glimpse of the assassin when he passed through a shaft of moonlight shining down through the trees. I went along cautiously, my revolver at the ready, my heart pounding.

Now we were only a few dozen yards behind the assassin. Now and then, I saw the glint of MacDuff's gun in the moonlight.

"I'm right behind you, MacDuff," I whispered. MacDuff nodded without turning around.

As we penetrated deeper into the woods the path grew narrower, the trees on either side of the path larger. The foliage grew thicker. Now the overhanging tree branches crisscrossing overhead shut out much of the moonlight. Now the path was a mere shadow twisting serpent-like through the woods in the night, and we were forced to slow our pace.

The assassin showed signs of fatigue. His footprints were closer together than before and there were scuffmarks on the path.

"We'll have him soon, Millicent," MacDuff whispered over his shoulder.

I stayed close behind MacDuff. I could, if I wished, reach out and touch his shoulder. We conversed quietly, a few words at a time, as we continued along the path.

Just then, the assassin stopped in his tracks. He spun around, looking for us. He now stood twenty yards away, clearly outlined against a shaft of moonlight streaming down through the trees. Crouching low he shaded his eyes with his hand, and looked in our direction.

"Get flat!" MacDuff hissed.

We both dropped face down on the cold damp earth. A shot rang out—then another! One of the bullets struck a tree nearby, making a loud thwack! The second bullet echoed through the woods, breaking twigs off branches.

"He's off and running again. Let's go, Millicent!"

When I stood up I saw the assassin ahead, a shadow among shadows.

Little pools of water began to appear, first on one side of the path, then on the other. Now the trees stood farther apart. The undergrowth gave way to thick bunches of reedy things. Soon, pools of water covered the path itself.

"He's heading straight into the swamp, Millicent." MacDuff said.

Now we were within fifteen yards of our quarry. In some of the low spots, the path was submerged. The assassin splashed noisily through the low places, MacDuff and I splashed through after him.

Little mounds of grass like little islands cropped up in what was now a swampy shallow lake of muddy water. The assassin used the mounds to pick his way through the mire. MacDuff and I picked our way using the same little islands.

Live trees now gave way to dead ones. The dead trees rose up out of the slimy waters bone-white, like skeletons rising from a watery grave. All around us was the foul odor of decay.

The assassin plodded on. MacDuff and I had now closed the gap considerably. Surely, we were no more than ten yards behind now.

Beyond where we stood there were no more little islands, no more high ground.

The assassin could go no farther into the swamp. He now had two choices. Stop and try to shoot us both, or give himself over in our custody.

MacDuff stopped. Placing a hand on my arm, he whispered, "Stay here, Millicent. I'm going to get closer. I'll tell him to throw down his gun. Probably he'll refuse, and then he'll try to kill me. If he shoots and I go down," MacDuff paused. "Well, you know what to do."

MacDuff was right. I knew what to do. A big tree stump nearby jutted waist-high out of the swamp water. The stump was old and rotten, but big enough to hide behind and thick enough to stop a bullet.

MacDuff put his hand on my shoulder. He looked at me for but a moment. Then he waded out into the swamp toward the assassin. The shallow water swirled round MacDuff's ankles. He moved closer to the mound of earth where the assassin stood waiting. Now the water came up to MacDuff's knees.

Without warning, the assassin leaped from the little piece of high ground, pistol in hand, and splashed farther into the swamp. MacDuff waded through the water and up onto the mound of earth occupied a moment ago by the assassin. The assassin stopped, spun quickly around and fired. MacDuff dropped to his knees in the nick of time, and the shot went wild. The assassin fired again. The gunshots echoed through the trees.

"Shoot him, MacDuff!" I shrieked.
MacDuff had flattened himself on the mound and was, again, unscathed. Then he stood up. I thought he must be crazy. MacDuff stood up and just stood there, calmly, with his revolver at his side, the barrel pointing at the muddy ground.

"Damn! Damn! Bloody Damn!" I hissed, crouching behind the stump. MacDuff stood between the assassin and me. All I could do was stand helplessly by until the assassin shot MacDuff down like a Coney Island sitting duck. Then, by god, I would bloody well blow the assassin's brains out!

I could not see the assassin's face because MacDuff was blocking my view, but over MacDuff's shoulder I saw his gun arm move, saw his shoulder rise up. Then the assassin leaned to the side. Just enough for me to see his face but not enough for a clear shot. There was on his face the smirk of anticipated victory.

Raising my head only enough, I rested the barrel of my revolver on top of the stump and took careful aim. I would squeeze the trigger the moment MacDuff fell. I took a breath and held it.

Snap! Snap!

"Oh my god," I yelled. Then I heard it again, loud, metallic, the loud snap you hear when somebody pulls the trigger on an empty gun.

"Damn you, MacDuff, and your half nigger woman!' the assassin shouted.

He threw the now impotent weapon at MacDuff, who easily ducked the missile. The gun flew past MacDuff's head, making a loud splash not far from where I stood by the stump.

"It's over," MacDuff said, his voice steady. "Put your arms above your head."

"Never!"

Reaching suddenly inside his coat the assassin snatched a second pistol from his belt, twin to the one he had discarded. An icy hand closed round my heart, my breathing stopped. MacDuff fired!

"Aiee!" The assassin's gun flew out of his hand, splashing into the muddy water behind him. He spun around, jumped off the piece of high ground, and groping with his left hand beneath the murky water began a frantic search for the gun. Failing to find it, he stood up, his bloody right hand hanging useless at his side.

"Give up," MacDuff said. "If you get a good lawyer, there's still a chance they won't hang you."

"Leave the gun where it is," I yelled.

Plunging his left arm back down into the swamp water, the assassin searched frantically once more for the gun. He wadded first one direction, then another in his futile search. He took one more step forward, then another longer step, and when he did he sank down to his waist. He tried stepping back, but couldn't. His forward leg was stuck. Having given up on the gun, he took hold of his leg with both hands and tried to pull it free. It only made matters worse. Shifting his weight drove the leg deeper into the mire.

The assassin's fate was now clear. In his final desperate search for the gun, he made a deadly error. He stepped into quicksand.

I couldn't believe it, but MacDuff attempted to save the man

"Roll on your back and lie flat, with your arms out to the side!" MacDuff shouted.

MacDuff jammed his own gun in his belt, and struggled out of his jacket. MacDuff would hold onto one of the sleeves, have the man grab onto the other sleeve, and then try to pull him free.

It was already too late. It was as though something strong, something merciless beneath the murky waters had grabbed hold of the assassin's leg. It was pulling him deeper down into the bog. Water now swirled round his chest. Then his arms and shoulders disappeared. Screaming and cursing, the assassin kept sinking, inch-by-inch down, down into the fetid, deadly netherworld of the Lily Dale swamp.

The man's screams and curses ceased abruptly, when the muddy gruel rose above his chin and poured into his gaping mouth. A choking sob was the last MacDuff and I heard from him. A writhing grasping hand slipping beneath the waters was the last we saw of him. It was the last anyone would ever see of him.

Chapter 36

"MacDuff, that was horrible!" I said.

MacDuff looked at me. His blue eye glittered.

"MacDuff," I said. "What in hell was that?"

"Uktena. That was my Grandfather's name for it, Millicent. He said it's a huge snake, big around as a tree trunk and real ugly. Hides in rivers, and in swamps like this. Grandfather said it has one thing on its mind. Vengeance, Millicent. Vengeance."

"Nemesis!" I said, remembering my classical mythology. "Goddess of Retribution."

MacDuff reached in his shirt pocket. He removed a leather pouch that I had seen before. Loosening the drawstring, MacDuff opened the pouch and withdrew a pinch of reddish powder, the same powder he used the day we discovered Eastman's body. MacDuff whispered some Cherokee words, and then he sprinkled the powder onto the place where the assassin's body sank. He said some more Cherokee words, and then sprinkled me with the powder. Finally, he sprinkled it on himself.

I was shivering. MacDuff put his arm round my shoulder. He tilted his head back and gazed up through the trees at the midnight sky.

"Look, Millicent," he said, pointing at a huge tree nearby.

It was an old dead tree without leaves or bark. It rose up out of the swamp a few yards beyond the quicksand. Perched atop the angular upper-most limb was an owl.

"Oh my god, MacDuff!" I said, shivering anew. Somehow, I was convinced that it was the same owl I saw when I got into that cab in Brooklyn; the same owl I saw at my window the first night MacDuff and I stayed at the Grand Hotel. The same owl.

Just then the owl spread its wings against the moon. It gave a series of long drawn-out hoots, rose from its perch, and glided away silently to the west.

MacDuff put his arm round my shoulder again, and again the shivers ceased. But, then, those other shivers set in. The ones that come upon me, suddenly, sometimes. When I reach round him to retrieve a book off a shelf behind his desk, and my hand inadvertently brushes his shoulder.

"MacDuff — about the Uktena."

"Yeah?"

"You don't actually believe that old myth. I mean, do you?"

"I never said it was a myth. I said it was a legend, Millicent."

"Oh, come on now, MacDuff. I know you better than that. You don't actually believe that creature is real."

"Uktena, lucky for us, she works for the Blind Lady, Millicent."

Chapter 37

Slowly we retraced our steps along the path, and walked out of the woods. I lifted my bag from under the bush where I had left it, and slung it over my shoulder.

We were weary. Yet, we could not just go back to our rooms at the Grand Hotel, and go to sleep. Now we had to go to Cornelia's house, where she and Miss Anthony, our two agents, and Melvin waited to know how the play ended. Not the Gilbert and Sullivan farce that opened the 1891 Fredonia Opera House first season. No, I mean the play that began in New York City ages ago, it now seemed, and ended tonight in the Lily Dale swamp.

Just before we left the stables, we searched the assassin's coach. We found a grip filled with men's medium size clothes.

"All packed up, and ready to go," I said.

Searching under the clothes, I found a letter.

"Look here, MacDuff," I said, showing him the letter.

We found a bench under a street lamp and sat down. I broke the black seal. The letter was dated the day before, and was addressed to MacDuff. We scanned the message.

"MacDuff," I said, "this will answer everybody's questions."

"Well, it answers everything I wanted to know."

"It was what the author was writing when we surprised him at the Grand Hotel," MacDuff said.

"Yes and what he pulled out of the typewriter carriage just before you broke down the door of room three forty-three."

I put the letter in my bag, and we trudged wearily to the Grand Hotel, to change into dry clothes before going to the Lassing-Tilton house in Melrose Park.

At the hotel, the night clerk said very excitedly as we went in the lobby, "Have you heard the news about the shooting at the Opera House!"

"No," we lied.

"Well, I've lived in and around these parts for forty years, and I've only seen one *Fredonia Sentinel* Extra before. It was when

President Lincoln was shot."

The clerk handed us the special edition. We took it to my room and read it.

Gunfire at the Opera House! Screamed the headline in the special edition of the *Sentinel*.

I mention only important highlights here. The article said that shots were fired tonight inside the Fredonia Opera House. 'The crazed gunman' then made a daring escape out the theater stage door. The article stressed that the gunman's identity was unknown. MacDuff and I were happy to note that neither Miss Anthony's nor Mrs. Lassing Tilton's name was even mentioned."

In the article, Police Chief Joseph Faber offered an explanation. Chief Faber said '…a great many wealthy people, the women wearing diamond necklaces, the men sprouting gold watches, attended the Fredonia Opera House Grand Opening.' Chief Faber said he thought the incident might have been … 'staged by a nihilist fanatic, to protest such an open display of wealth.'

MacDuff and I hoped the story would still make sense to the police in the morning. It did give us both a chuckle.

MacDuff went to his room to change into dry clothes; I went to my room to do the same.

Chapter 38

On our way from the Grand to the Lassing-Tilton residence, we came upon Emma Goldberg sitting on a bench in Melrose Park, under a streetlamp. We walked up to Miss Goldberg and sat down with her, one on either side. Emma had been crying. She looked at me with tears in her eyes.

"What is it, Emma?" I said. "What has happened?"

She held an envelope out to me.

"Under my door, I find this when I go to room now."

So many letters, so much bad news, I thought to myself.

"From my Sasha," Emma said, crying still. "You will to read?" Emma said.

I took the envelope. Black sealing wax had been used. I opened the envelope, withdrew the brief message. I read the letter. MacDuff read it over my shoulder.

"My stupid little Jewess," the letter began. It then went on to say that by the time Emma read the letter, Miss Anthony would be dead and he, Alexander Berkholdt, would be on his way out of the country with a new identity, and a great deal of money waiting for him in a European bank. The letter ended with: "Whatever made you think that I, Alexander Berkholdt, one of the Master Race, could love a Jew woman, one of Herr Nietzsche's bungled and botched. Bah!' I merely needed you to complete my anarchist disguise."

The letter was shorter, but some of the content was much the same as what Berkholdt had written in his final letter to us.

Emma sobbed till I thought her heart would surely break. I put my arm around her, and she cried into my shoulder. She told us how Berkholdt had lied to her from the very beginning, telling her that he was an anarchist who fled from Tsarist Russia to escape being hanged for a murder that he did not commit. Berkholdt told Emma he was even now afraid for his life. She took him into her house, and then, she said, into her heart. No one would doubt his anarchist identity with Emma Goldberg at his side.

Emma helped to dispel for us some of the mystery surrounding the events that night at Justice Schwab's Saloon. For example, she told us she was certain it had been Berkholdt who had tried to run over MacDuff that night, when she and Berkholdt ran out of Justice Schwab's back door. Berkholdt had sent Emma home in a cab, saying he would see her at the apartment later. Emma said Berkholdt did not come home until early next morning, and would not tell her where he had been or what he had been doing.

We told Emma that we, too, had received another letter from Berkholdt. In the letter, Berkholdt also admitted to being the one who plotted to kill Miss Anthony.

"Now I know why Sasha receive letters from Germany, and wrote letters back. About these letters, he would not to tell me."

We told Emma what had happened to Berkholdt in the Lily Dale swamp. Overall she handled it well.

Chapter 39

At first Miss Goldberg did not want to go with us to the Lassing Tilton house, where we would have to retell the story to the others. She felt she could not endure the embarrassment. But upon further consideration, she felt she should go with us.

All the other houses bordering the park were dark. At Cornelia's house, a single dim lamp glowed in the parlor window. We walked up onto the porch, and MacDuff knocked on the door. The curtain moved at the parlor window. Something metallic poking out between the window casing and the curtain caught the light of the lamp, and then disappeared.

A deadbolt slammed back, the door flew open. In the doorway stood Billy Bergin, legs set wide apart, arms straight out, both hands gripping a gun, the gun pointing at MacDuff's chest. We heard footsteps behind us. Dixon, on the porch.

"Okay, Billy. You too, Dixon," MacDuff glanced over his shoulder. "Holster your guns, the show's over."

"Sorry about the gun-point welcome, MacDuff," Billy said, "but we couldn't take a chance."

We went inside, and received a warm greeting from everyone.

There was another person in the room whose presence MacDuff and I hadn't anticipated. Mrs. Isabella Beecher Hooker. Belle's train had suffered a derailment near Syracuse. She arrived in Lily Dale just minutes after Miss Anthony and Cornelia returned from the opera.

Belle ran up to us and exclaimed, "Oh! Oh! I am so happy to see you both. And unharmed!"

She hugged both of us, and then sat down next to Miss Anthony. She reached over and gave Miss Anthony's hand a squeeze.

Billy and Dixon drew chairs from the dining room, and made a half circle of them at the front end of the parlor. MacDuff and I sat down next to each other; Emma sat cross-legged on the floor by me. Miss Anthony occupied the chair across from us, by the window. Cornelia went to the kitchen to get the teacart.

"Please," Belle said, looking at MacDuff, then at me. "Do

tell us everything."

"Before you begin," Cornelia interrupted, having returned with the cart and some freshly brewed tea. "I want to say," Cornelia looked at MacDuff, Billy, Dixon, and me. "If it weren't for all of you, surely Miss Anthony would have been killed tonight." Cornelia paused. "And so might I have been!" Her hand shook picking up her tea.

"Now please, Belle said, "do tell us everything."

Taking turns, MacDuff and I told our story. We described, in detail, what had happened since Belle hired us, and then we read the letter that we found in the assassin's grip.

"This letter was the last in a series of letters written to us by the assassin while we chased him across New York State, from Brooklyn all the way to Lily Dale. The letter answers all of the questions that have baffled us ever since MacDuff and I took on the case. This letter written by Alexander Berkholdt will answer all of your questions too."

I read the letter.

"My dear Mr. MacDuff, when Miss Anthony steps up to the podium tomorrow, she will have given her last speech; for, you see, I am going to kill her. She will die before the coming week begins. And if you and your precious Millicent aren't just ever so careful, both of you will also die. In any case, by the time you read this -- if you are still alive, that is -- the deed will have been done. Miss Anthony will be dead, and I shall be on my way out of the country, with a great deal of money waiting for me in a European bank, and I shall have a new identity.

"And why must Miss Anthony die? Surely you wonder. Miss Anthony, you see, believes as strongly in her cause as I believe in mine. As a Suffrage worker she would do anything to win the right for women to vote. Unfortunately, however, Miss Anthony would enfranchise even the poor, the ignorant, the weak -- Herr Nietzsche's bungled and botched'. But our planners, dear Mr. MacDuff, foresee an end to your kind

before the 50th year of the coming century, when the Master Race shall prevail. And I, Alexander Berkholdt, would do anything to assure its success.

"It is unfortunate that Miss Anthony must die. Because for a woman she is rather intelligent, and stripped of her stupid beliefs she would make excellent female stock for our breeding farm in Germany, my native land. That is, of course, if she were considerably younger."

The letter ended. MacDuff had interrupted the writer by breaking down his door.

No one interrupted me while I read. Now everyone sat very quietly, thinking about what I had just shared with them.

"Well, he was no crackpot," Cornelia said. "And not one of those crazy anarchists, either."

Emma Goldberg squirmed in her chair.

"No. He wasn't an anarchist," MacDuff said. "That was just a cover, another mask to hide behind. But he was a strong believer in Eugenics."

These Eugenicists," Belle said. "What, exactly, is their ultimate goal?"

"The ultimate goal of Eugenics, I said, "as I understand it, is to create a so called Master Race using selective breeding."

I explained what was meant by selective breeding.

"Miss Millicent?" Dixon had a look on his face just then which I would describe as a mixture of profound sadness and intense anger.

"Yes, Mr. Dixon," I said.

"With all respect, Miss Millicent, I heard from this here head doctor on Blackwell's Island, that there's a faster way to do that -- to create some kinda Master Race," Dixon said.

"Please, Dixon, go on," I said.

Dixon cleared his throat nervously.

"When I was a kid I got in trouble, see?" Dixon caught Miss Anthony's eye. "I was a dip, Miss Anthony, a pickpocket. It's how I lived from when I was about eight years old. That's when my mom and pop died of the influenza." Dixon paused. He squirmed in his chair, and then continued. "I stold somebody's wallet." Dixon paused.

"I gotta be honest with yaz." Dixon, red-faced, scanned the other faces in the room. "I stold a lotta wallets. But I got caught stealing this one wallet, see, when I was 'bout thirteen. So the coppers, they sent me to The Island for a stretch, you know, Blackwell's Island, where they send NY City kids that goes wrong. MacDuff was there once, wasn't you, MacDuff?"

MacDuff rolled his eyes. Miss Anthony grinned ever so slightly.

"Well," Dixon continued, "there was this head-doctor on Blackwell's Island when I was there, who had this idea 'bout how to fix why kids go bad. He said that one day they, meaning him and other guys like him, was gonna round up all the pickpockets like me, and all the gangsters and all the poor people and all the people what drank too much, and anybody what had some kinda what he called defects, which he said was most of the immigrant people that came here and all the Indians that was already here and all the black people that was brought here as slaves, and they was gonna put us all in one place like Blackwell's Island…and then… and then … kill us all."

Dixon laughed. It was the saddest little laugh I have ever heard.

"He said they was going to kill us all in a humane kinda way so nobody'd suffer. You know, by usin' the kinda gas what kills coal miners. He said everybody'd jist go to sleep, and never wake up."

"And then, this here head-doctor said, there wouldn't be no more problems with kids like me what end up being pickpockets, or with people what had these here defects he talked about. You remember that doctor on the Island, MacDuff?"

"I remember him alright," MacDuff said.

Many long minutes passed. Billy Bergin broke the silence. "But why did Alexander Berkholdt want to kill Miss Anthony?" Billy looked at her. "There's nothing wrong with you, Miss

Anthony."

Miss Anthony smiled behind her hand.

"No, there's nothing wrong with Miss Anthony, Billy," MacDuff said.

Again the group grew silent, again long minutes passed.

"I'm afraid I still don't understand why Miss Anthony became a target for assassination by these radical Eugenicists," Cornelia said.

"Alexander Berkholdt believed that the Suffrage Movement stood in the way of the goal set by the Eugenicists," I said, "and, of course, he was right. Miss Anthony, I believe you have always stood against Eugenics?"

"I most certainly have!" Miss Anthony's face flared.

"And because of your influence in this country, you're a threat to Eugenics," I said, "and in their minds you stand in the way of their ultimate goal.

"Women, as a group, are far more liberal than their male counterparts. Should they acquire the right to vote, women would become the most powerful liberal force in the country, and would cast their votes for liberal causes. Unfortunately, our government is now run by men who think more or less like Alexander Berkholdt. They are against equal rights, against trade unions, against charity for the poor, and other liberal causes. These same greedy men are very much afraid, that if Suffrage succeeds it would mean the end to their power -- and they are right, Miss Anthony, isn't that so?"

Miss Anthony smiled that small, thin smile.

"Absolutely," she said.

"And that's why Alexander Berkholdt tried to kill you," MacDuff said.

Long minutes passed, as each person tried to come to terms with what had just been said.

Finally, Belle spoke up.

"But neither of you have as yet told us exactly what happened to Alexander Berkholdt," Belle said. "Has he already been turned over to the police?"

Miss Anthony's posture stiffened. Her lips grew pale.

MacDuff looked at me.

"No, Belle," I said. "The assassin is not in police custody. He is, well." The words would not come out.

MacDuff stood up. He looked at each person in Cornelia's little parlor, all of them eager to hear what had become of the man who tried to assassinate Miss Susan B. Anthony. He looked at each person, in turn, for a full minute, using only that cold blue eye shining like gunmetal in the lamplight. MacDuff cleared his throat. He spoke slowly and clearly.

"Alexander Berkholdt is at the bottom of a quicksand bog in the Lily Dale swamp."

Everyone in the circle was properly aghast. We explained, briefly, how it happened, and why it would be virtually impossible to locate Berkholdt's body. Then Melvin spoke:

"I know an old Indian that's got a camp back in those woods, calls himself Oskotonta. And he says there's places in that Lily Dale swamp that ain't even got a bottom."

"Now that we know what happened to Alexander Berkholdt, shouldn't we do something now?" Cornelia said. "I mean, shouldn't we inform the police?"

Miss Anthony stiffened. Belle took in a sudden breath. Miss Emma Goldberg swore into her hand.

MacDuff stood and faced the group.

"Should we, as Cornelia suggests, go to the police and tell them what happened tonight?"

MacDuff planted his feet firmly against the floor.

"To my ancestors, and to me, a promise is sacred. When Millicent and I took on this case, we made a promise to Belle, our client, and later we made the same promise to Miss Anthony. Miss Millicent and I promised that we would not, under any circumstances, say anything to the press, or to the official police about the plot to kill Miss Anthony, even if somebody actually tried to kill her.

"As you know somebody did try to kill Miss Anthony."

MacDuff shot a glance at me. "Some Opening Night, huh, Millicent?"

No one laughed.

MacDuff paused. The group waited.

"Luckily, the attempt failed," he said.

Everyone looked at Miss Anthony. MacDuff clapped his hands together lightly, in muted applause. We all joined in. Miss Anthony blushed.

"As you now know, the man who tried to kill Miss Anthony is at the bottom of the Lily Dale swamp," MacDuff continued, his voice growing louder now. "No one knows this but us, the people in this room. If Millicent and I tell the police, it would break our promise to Belle our client, and to Miss Anthony the intended victim of the plot. Of course, the police would inform the press.

"Millicent and I agree with both our client and Miss Anthony. If knowledge of the plot reaches the public, even though the plot failed, there's a good chance that Women's Suffrage which Miss Anthony has fought so hard for all her life, will die. More power will fall into the hands of people like Alexander Berkholdt!"

"Also," Billy piped up, "any publicity about the assassination attempt could lead to what the cops call a 'copycat crime.' Somebody else could get the idea that, if he tried, he wouldn't fail. It would put Miss Anthony's life at risk again."

"MacDuff is right," I pleaded. "We mustn't inform the police. I beg of you, tell no one, not even your families, about what happened in the Lily Dale swamp; tell no one what was said here tonight. Let what was said in this room be left unsaid in the history books.

"I, for one, shall never speak of it to another soul as long as I live," I said forcefully.

"Nor will I," MacDuff said, striking his palm with his fist.

"What plot?" Billy said. "If you ask me, there wasn't any plot to kill Miss Anthony."

"Let Berkholdt rot in that quicksand hole," Dixon said, "with no one to know he's there, an' no one to put flowers on his grave. Guys like Berkholdt, they don't deserve nothin' better!"

"I shall tell no one," said Cornelia.

"I wouldn't think of it," said Belle, smiling at her life-long friend and fellow Suffragist.

All eyes turned to Melvin. He poked at the carpet with the toe of his boot, scratched the stubble on his chin.

"Course I won't say nothin," Melvin said. "Who the hell would believe me?"

Emma Goldberg, the last to speak, stood up to face the group.

"There is something to Miss Anthony I must now say." Emma stared at the floor.

"I too receive letter today, Miss Anthony. From Alexander Berkholdt."

She had the letter in her hand, and she read from it.

"In letter, Berkholdt said: 'Whatever makes you think that I, Alexander Berkholdt, one of the Master Race, could ever love a stupid little Jew woman?' He say he only needed me to complete his Anarchist disguise."

Suddenly, she could hold back no longer. She turned once more to face Miss Anthony, and blurted out:

"Oh, Miss Anthony, I am so ashamed! Alexander Berkholdt, I was his lover!

"But I swear, Miss Anthony, he lie to me from very beginning. Not until today did I know he would try to kill you."

Emotionally exhausted, Emma could say no more.

MacDuff and I stood up and addressed the group. "It's true," I said. "MacDuff and I read the letter Berkholdt wrote to her. She knew nothing about the plot until she read the letter."

"It is true," MacDuff said.

Emma collapsed onto a chair. Miss Anthony and Belle looked at her. Emma looked away, embarrassed and ashamed. Rising from her chair, Miss Anthony walked over and stood facing Emma. She took Emma's hand in hers, gently. Then she said loud enough for all to hear:

"Miss Goldberg," Miss Anthony said, "Belle and I are sure that you knew nothing of the plot."

Emma nodded gratefully. Miss Anthony went back and sat down. Emma stood up.

Then tearfully, through her anger and her grief, Emma Goldberg said:

"I spit on Alexander Berkholdt's grave."

Made in the USA
Charleston, SC
23 June 2015